A Choice: Book I

A Choice: Book I

The Chosen Hybrid Series

Sharuthie Ramesh

Library of Congress Control Number:		2014906073
ISBN:	Hardcover	978-1-4931-9634-0
	Softcover	978-1-4931-9635-7
	eBook	978-1-4931-9633-3

This is a work of fiction. Names, characters, places and incidents either are the product of the author's imagination or are used fictitiously, and any resemblance to any actual persons, living or dead, events, or locales is entirely coincidental.

Printed in the United States of America by BookMasters, Inc
Ashland OH
June 2014

Rev. date: 06/17/2014

To order additional copies of this book, contact:
Xlibris LLC
1-888-795-4274
www.Xlibris.com
Orders@Xlibris.com
542009

To my dad, who always works so hard, and always gets whatever my eyes see, and to my mom, for always being there for me and never letting me out of her sight (literally!). This book wouldn t have been made without the help of Xlibris, but the book wouldn t have a story without my family and friends! Stay Pure!

Contents

CHAPTER 1

Kyra

YOU KNOW, BEING a princess isn't that easy.

You would have to take care of an entire country. And the worst part is having to learn how to be one all by yourself. Ever since my parents and my dear sister, Bethela, were murdered in the biggest war of all, I've had the entire Mortal Portal country lying on my shoulders. It was very lonely. Of course, it wasn't long until I was at crossroads, which changed my fate in as many ways possible, and I wasn't alone after that. I am going to tell you a story about love, changes, and choices. It all started a few months after my 118th birthday and after the war that changed my life . . .

I was under my favorite willow tree, the sun beaming on my yellow dress that brought out my light gray eyes, complementing my curvy body. The wind was calm, with only a light breeze that blew my dark wavy hair. It was a sunny spring day, and I was plucking flower petals off a tulip when I noticed something. It was quiet. Too quiet. All of the sudden, a heart-stopping scream pierced the air. I saw one of the stable boys run toward me. "Your Highness! Your Highness!" he yelled, panicked. "Come quick! Aries has come to kill us all!"

Now that's not something you hear every day. I guess that's what I get for being born in a royal family on a planet called T-Residents. Yep, I'm the princess of the Mortal Portal country and no one on Earth knows about me or everyone else on this planet. Of course, I visited Earth a few times, so I know about humans, but people like me don't want to come to Earth often because many people believe our race is dangerous. And we could be dangerous.

"I'll be right there." I got to my feet and ran to the Mortal Portal castle, my "house." When I got there, everybody was in panic. I put two fingers in my mouth and let out a high-pitched whistle, causing everybody to stop and to stare at me. I looked at one of my servants, a skinny hobgoblin girl named Curela, and asked her where Aries was. With a shaky finger, she pointed toward the meeting hall, where I held war meetings. Thanking her, I dashed to the meeting hall and threw open the doors to find Aries Deatheye sitting on my father's throne.

He wore a business suit with a midnight blue tie though it didn't seem right for the occasion. He appeared to have not changed at all since the war. His short hair dark as the night, his muscles hard as stone, he wore a smile on his stubborn mouth, and his eyes were simmering black like the hell he had went through.

The second he saw me, he grinned as I slammed the door shut and locked it behind me, turning to face him with a serious look upon my face. "Hello, Kyra. Nice place you've got here." He gestured grandly around the room.

"Thank you, Lord Aries. I feel honored to be standing in front of the great demon himself," I said in a sarcastic tone, hinting that I wasn't in the mood.

"Why, you know flattering won't get you anywhere."

I hated when he pretended that he couldn't notice that I wasn't in the mood for jokes. "Spill it, Aries. I'm really tired and I'm not up for a fight today. Besides, the answer's no if you're asking me to swear loyalty to you." I wasn't high on being formal with many people. Plus, I had no idea why Aries was there. It had been a few months since the last war ended, and we finally declared peace until further notice. So it made no sense why he was here.

His smile was replaced by a menacing grin. "Why, I'm not here for that." His laughter rang throughout the room. I was as confused as the look on my face. "You really don't know, do you?" He laughed. "Why, I'm here for one reason only."

I rolled my eyes at the demi demon. *What does he want,* I wondered. "Just tell me what you want! There's no need for this useless game! State your business and leave to your kingdom!"

He shook his head, disappointed. "I truly thought you've heard the news. But I guess I'll have to tell you now." He sighed.

I felt fear come over me. *Oh, God, please not something worse,* I prayed. But I had no idea what was coming.

He got up off the throne and walked toward me until he was so close, our bodies almost touched. I resisted the urge to take a step back, and instead, I stared him dead in the eyes. He talked in a low voice. "Kyra Rumblen Count. I know this sounds crazy, but will you marry one of my sons?"

CHAPTER 2

The Deal

"EXCUSE ME?" I asked, shocked to the core, as I jumped back. Aries, my sworn enemy since birth, killer of my family, was asking me to marry one of his offsprings. How confusing it was to hear *that* coming out of his mouth.

"I asked if you'd marry one of my sons," he said calmly. "Not me. You'll be surprised." He added with a chuckle, "They are very handsome."

"No way! I'd rather be killed than marry one of your boys. I don't want to have to deal with more than one Aries!" I started to glare at him, but then stopped. There was something in his eyes. Sorrow, guilt, and most of all, embarrassment. Embarrassed that the princess of the MP declined one of his son's for marriage. His mouth went grim. The room had just gotten bigger, causing me to feel even smaller with Aries's presence in the room.

He cleared his voice. "Listen. I know we've had a rough history, and I know that you'll never forgive me for what I've done. But at least come to my castle and meet my sons. Talk to them, be friends with them, and later you can decide whom you want to marry. Ever since Luna died " – his voice started to shake – " you know it's been hard on me and even harder on the boys. With a woman in the house, we'll be complete, and it'll bring peace between us." He stared at me expecting me to say yes, hope glint in his eyes.

And the thing is I actually wanted to. I felt bad for him. Luna, his wife, was beautiful and the sweetest thing I've ever met. Her personality matched her dark gray eyes, her dark curls, and she was a vampire like me. Even though the fight separated us, we used to meet up secretly and braid each other's hair and talk about life. She taught me everything I needed to know in order to rule the MP. She was like a second mother. Plus, we looked strangely alike. It's a pity she died brutally. Stabbed in the heart with a wooden stake by one of my men in the last war. Ever since, I've had always seen sadness in Aries's eyes. So I stood there wondering what to do. Marry a demon's offspring or keep this war going? I sighed. "What if I say no?" I dared to ask.

Aries's face darkened. "Then I'll kill everybody. Not you, but all of your people, piece by piece, limb by limb. And I'll make you regret saying no." He was dead serious. Clearly, that spoke the truth.

I gulped, knowing that he wasn't bluffing. "Then you're giving me no choice but to marry one of your sons?"

"When you put it like that, then yes. You have no choice." He smiled, his pearly white teeth showing.

I groaned. "All right. I'll meet your sons and then decide. But you know this will take some time, right? I mean, if I am to get married to one of them, I should at least build a friendship with them."

"So we have a deal?" He grinned, happy that he won. He put out his hand.

"I guess we do," I said as we shook on it. I couldn't help but felt as if I made a huge mistake. After, he told me that he'd pick me up at midnight, enough time so I can tell the kingdom the news and pack. I was nervous. I had to leave my kingdom vulnerable, just so I can get married. Wow. Being 118 years old meant that I was ready for marriage. And to become a queen, I needed to marry. Because if there was a queen, there needed to be a king. I've always dreaded the thought of marriage. I didn't believe in love ever since I lost my parents and sister. It's one of the most dangerous types of human emotion and it's heightened for hybrids.

Anyways, after we shook hands, Aries unlocked the doors and threw them open to find many faces of servants peering up at him in horror. Silently, they let Aries through, and soon, he was out the front door on his way to his kingdom. I told the palace my plan, which caused several to faint and others to cry out in fear, and I decided to put Arwin in charge. Arwin Vansiv was my dearest friend and a unicorn, though she always stayed in human form, not horse form, and she was slightly skinnier than me and taller. She had big brown eyes that can change into any color that suits her mood, which matched her flowing brown hair that went over her shoulders. Though she was two years older than me, she acted my age. She was ravishing and a healer. Though she mostly came on holidays, she told me that she'd stay and keep an eye on the kingdom until I came back. If I came back of course. As I packed, I made sure that I brought everything I needed: my clothing, my undergarments, my spell book, my wand, my lucky dragon tooth, magic case that contained every spell or potion ingredient, my crusader sword, my daggers and knives, my phone, laptop, and my precious item, my soul bag. In my soul bag, I kept everything I've earned from training: Fire stone, Water stone, Earth stone, Air stone, my spirit (a bat) stone, and a fallen star. I also had my family's soul rocks and mine. If I lost that bag, I would be left with no power and vulnerable to anybody and anything. So I made sure to put a spell lock on my luggage so nothing can break into it. I, then, changed into an orange tank top and my favorite denim skinny jeans, my hair held up in a ponytail. After, I went outside and waited for midnight.

It was 10:00 p.m, when I heard footsteps, then a *thump*, and a curse followed after it. "Hello?" I called. Silence pierced the night. I got off the stairs and went to the willow tree. I used to stay there and think. It was a very quiet night and I was the only one outside. I was all alone and vulnerable. I had left my luggage on the porch. I sat under the willow tree's protection. The moon was full and I felt power surge through me, its light illuminating my striking features. The only light there was the moon's rays and the village's lampposts faintly in the distance. I sat there admiring my kingdom, knowing that it might be the last thing I see of it for a while. It was so quiet; I felt a chill come over me. As if I was being watched. As if I wasn't alone. I looked around. Not a soul in sight. Not trusting my sight, I sniffed the air. No blood. Not even the beating of a heart. I lay down against the willow's trunk. I was about to drift to sleep when a hand clamped over my mouth.

CHAPTER 3

Gustav

I TRIED TO wrestle the hand off my mouth. Not to cry for help, but to wrestle the fool. My captor removed his hand, clamping it on my arm and dragged me to the other side of the tree. He backed me up until my back was against the tree's trunk. He pinned my arms above my head with one arm and clamped the other on my mouth again. He leaned in so close to my face I could smell the blood and mint in his breath. "Struggling won't help you," he said in a low voice. My captor was surprisingly strong and fast, and he looked about my age, possibly older. His dark brown hair was short; his bangs slightly covered his eyes. He had a strong jawline and a smile that only meant trouble. His eyes were a startling icy blue, sucking away my energy. He appeared to be wearing classic war gear, though the leather jacket's sleeves were cut off and hung open, exposing his black-and-blue striped shirt. I saw that he had blood marks on his hands and shirt. He examined me, head and down. "I won't hurt you since you're a ravishing girl, unless you don't tell me where your princess is." His mocking tone was strangely familiar.

I stood there, confused, and then it hit me. *He doesn't know it's me*, I realized. He, then, removed his hand from my mouth and braced it lightly against my neck. His eyes flashed wickedly.

"Spill it. Which room does Princess Count stay in?" His mouth gone grim. When I didn't reply, he added, "You don't want to feel the pain I can give you.

Besides, I can't tire myself out trying to wrestle information out of you. I need to save my energy to kick her little highness's butt."

I smiled up at him, as if to challenge him. "Why would you want to kick my butt?" He appeared surprised by my forwardness, and then realizing what was going on, he grinned. His grip tightened on my neck and I winced at his strength.

"Why, it's you, isn't it? Hello, Kyra Rumblen Count. I didn't even notice you in skinny jeans and a tank top." Then, he smacked his forehead dramatically. "Damn it! I forgot my manners. I am Gustav. Gustav Deatheye, eldest son of Aries and Luna Deatheye. You've met my father, haven't you?" He smiled, boyish and handsome, but there was a dark edge to it.

My heart dropped. This was Aries's son. One of my marrying options. "You were joking before, right? Your father must have sent you. My luggage is in the front. Where did you park?" I turned my head, looking for any sign of how he had gotten to where I was. Then, it hit me. "You are here to pick me up, right?"

He had a puzzled look on his face. That wasn't the look I was looking for or hoping for. Then, he started to laugh. "Are you kidding? Why would I pick you up? Why, I've come to kill you." His eyes twinkled. "I'm going to enjoy this." He shoved me to the ground so fast it seemed to happen in a blur. He was quick to pounce on top of me. I struggled under him, but he was his father's son. His strength was frightening. He wasn't hesitant to lock his hands over my throat. He didn't squeeze hard, so I could still breathe and talk. I clawed at his hands but it didn't make a difference. I stared up at him with rage. He grinned. "You know, I thought that you'd be harder to take down. I guess you're no match for me."

"Don't let that ego get to your head," I warned him. "It'll cost you. Besides, if you weren't on me right now, I could have beaten you already. Sorry to pop your bubble." I knew reverse psychology worked in movies, but I hoped that it worked in real life. And it did.

His grin deepened. "Really? Okay then," he said. "I'll get off you and give you three seconds to get ready and fight me. Ready?" He got off me and I jumped to my feet. "Three . . . ," he started, but I didn't wait to hear what came next. I ran. Into the woods. I knew it was such a cowardly thing to do, but for once, instead of fighting, I wanted to get away from that maniac. I was scared for my life, and my heart was beating fast. "Two . . . ," Gustav yelled, not even chasing me, not even trying to stop me. I was so tired, running at vampire's speed, not wanting to hear. "One . . . Ready or not, here I come!" All of a sudden, I wasn't tired and so I ran for my life. I heard him running. A minute later he was right behind me. His breath was icy cold and he didn't seem tired. "Is that as fast as you can go?" he hollered behind me. I saw a deep drop up ahcad and then realized that we were heading for the war field behind the castle. There was a massive drop. I was sure Gustav had no idea about this, but then I heard him halt. I kept running. When I was a few steps away from the drop, I started focus on becoming a bat.

"Bat, bat, bat! C'mon, change into a bat, dammit!" I urged myself, muttering under my breath. That was when I started to change forms into a bat. Since I'm a hybrid, a powerful one, I possess all powers of all creatures known, and since my vamp side is stronger, I can easily change into a bat and unleash my fangs faster. So I took flight as a bat and soared back to my palace, leaving Gustav to find his own way home. When I got back to the front where my bags were, I found out that someone was waiting for me.

CHAPTER 4

Bonzai

A DARK FIGURE was waiting for me, next to my bags, his back facing me. "Who are you? Leave at once or face the consequences!" I warned this stranger, my fangs shot out. He spun around, startled.

"Princess Count? Why, I've been looking everywhere for you!" the figure exclaimed. "Don't just stand there! Turn yourself into a bat and I'll get your things."

I studied him. He looked like he was 118, like me. Dark brown hair laid low on his forehead, his muscles rippled through his blue T-shirt, and he wore denim jeans and Nikes. He had a strong jaw and wore an impatient scowl on his attractive face. But his eyes seemed to be the most attractive part about him. They were green, emerald green. He had a boyish charm in them that made him look irresistible. He too was oddly familiar, like a certain person I knew, and I found myself oddly attracted to him. I stared at him, not knowing what he was talking about. Then it had hit me. This figure was here to take me to Xercus. Aries's castle. Yet, I stood my ground and decided to test the stranger. "Who are you," I repeated, "and why are you here?"

He studied me and then realized that I was waiting for his reply. "I am Bonzai Deatheye, son of Luna Deatheye and stepson of Aries Deatheye. My stepfather told me that you have accepted the proposal and I needed to pick you up. Happy?"

I stared back at him and relaxed a little. He looked like his mother, soft with the exception of some muscles. "It's nice to meet you, Bonzai. You look like your mother." I paused. "I'm so sorry about the loss. She was my dearest friend and she taught me everything. It's an honor to see that her genes have been passed onto you." I forced my fangs back into their slots and smiled.

He smiled at me for a second, but it was soon replaced with a growl. He jumped in front of me as if to protect me. He sniffed the air. "Princess Count – "

"Please. Call me Kyra," I interrupted.

"All right. Kyra, we have some company. Do you know how to fight?"

"Of course I do! Who doesn't?"

"In case I fail you, run. Okay?"

I stared at him as if he was the dumbest person I had ever met. "I'm sorry but I cannot. As princess, I need to defend myself and the people around me."

He ignored me and faced forward. "I know someone's there. Show yourself and no harm will come to you," he called out. There were footsteps, heading toward us. He pulled out a dagger and bared his teeth. His sharp teeth.

I gasped. "You're a vampire too," I said, awed.

"Not now," he growled as he faced to the woods. A figure emerged from the misty woods. I shivered. It was Gustav.

He came closer and grinned. "Hello, little brother. I see you've found my prey. Would you like to hand her over? I have some unfinished work with this one." He took a step closer, his gaze on me, and he shot me a dazzling grin that would have wooed me if I weren't on his kill list.

Bonzai narrowed his eyes at his brother. "What are you doing here? Aries didn't send you here to pick her up. He sent me."

Gustav groaned. "Come on. Let me rough her up before we kidnap her! I've been chasing her until she turned into a damn bat! Not everyone's a vamp like you!" He scowled at his brother's fangs.

Bonzai looked confused, but still sucked his fangs back. "What *are* you here for, really?"

"I'm here to kill the girl that murdered our mother!" Gustav yelled. His eyes were icy light blue, filled with fury. "How dare you let her live? Her army killed our mother and I demand justice! If you're too weak to kill her, I will!" And just like that, he attacked. He charged towards us, full speed. He looked ready to kill.

Bonzai kicked his brother back and Gustav fell. Bonzai was on him in a second, pinning his hands above his head. His green eyes appeared calm, but there was a hint of confusion. "I cannot let you hurt her. We must bring her to the castle unharmed. That's what your father told me to do." He paused, realizing what was going on. "You don't know, do you?"

He sneered. "I know that my brother's a traitor."

Bonzai shook his head, impatiently. "Gustav, she's our bride-to-be! One of us is going to marry her!"

CHAPTER 5

Misunderstandings

GUSTAV WAS SO shocked; he fainted. I wasn't sure if I should have been insulted or relieved that he fainted at the news. Bonzai got off his brother and picked him up. He looked at me. "I'm sorry. Gustav didn't hear the news. He was away on a hunting trip, and our eldest brother didn't tell him. He's just angry about what has happened." His eyes showed how ashamed he was. I felt bad for Bonzai.

I placed my hand on his shoulder. "It's all right. I was angry at your father for killing my family." I smiled at him. "You were really brave to stand up to your brother. He reminds me of your father."

"Stepfather," he corrected. "He will never be my father and he knows it." He started to turn away, but he stopped. He sniffed the air. "Speaking of the devil," he swore.

Headlights grew brighter toward us. The silver SUV came to a screeching halt. The driver jumped out and ran to us. It was Aries, my soon-to-be father-in-law. I heard Bonzai groan. I did too at the same time. Aries looked ready to kill. He stopped in front of us, taking a minute to register the scene: Bonzai carrying Gustav, Gustav unconscious covered in dirt and blood, and me, covered in dirt, a hand on Bonzai's shoulder. After he took in the scene before him, he spoke. "Hello, Princess," he said to me. "I'm sorry you had to wait for Bonzai. He can be very forgetful and useless. As for Gustav, I take it he didn't know about our deal?"

"Aries," Bonzai said, annoyed of Aries's presence, "Darq didn't tell him the news, and so Gustav decided to kill Her Highness. I was waiting here for an hour until her Highness came covered in dirt. After a few minutes, Gustav decided to make a point to me that the princess was his prey and then he tried to attack her. So I tackled him and when I told him the news, he fainted."

Aries looked at Bonzai, a cold look on his face. "Put down your brother. He should walk to the car."

Bonzai looked hesitant but followed his orders. He placed his brother on the ground and then took out a bottle of water from a bag I didn't see before. He then poured the water on Gustav's face. Gustav shot up on his feet, teeth bared, eyes enraged. But as soon as he saw his father, he was quick to dust himself off. "Father, you came at the right time," he pointed to Bonzai. "Bonzai was trying to convince me that this girl is our bride-to-be!"

His father looked at me. "I apologize, Kyra. Gustav can be so clueless at times." He then turned to his confused son. "Gustav, it appears that Darq still hasn't informed you about Kyra. She will be staying with us until she has made her decision." He finally turned to Bonzai. "Get her bags and yourself into the car."

Bonzai nodded and then grabbed my bags and headed to the SUV. Aries turned and walked to the driver's side, leaving Gustav and me. I let out a sigh and looked at Gustav. "Listen, I think we weren't thinking about what we said to each other before. I just wanted to say that I look forward to liv – "

"Shut up!" Gustav said, not looking at me, with an icy voice. "Maybe what you said before you didn't mean. But that doesn't go for me. I meant every word." He turned and came closer to me and whispered into my ear. "I will not stop torturing you until I have you on your knees, begging me for mercy." He walked away to the car, leaving me with a stunned expression on my face. *Oh god,* I thought with a groan and a shiver. I headed to the SUV and opened the back door. I sat on the left and Bonzai sat on the right. Gustav sat up in the front with his father who was driving. We were all silent for the entire car ride. I looked out the window the entire time, watching my now-vulnerable country slip away and was thinking what would I do at Xercus.

CHAPTER 6

Xercus

IT WAS AN hour ride, and when I was about to give in to sleep, Aries called my name from the front. "Welcome to your new home, Kyra." I looked out the window and was astonished. It was a graveyard, except the people in the graves weren't in their graves. They roamed the area as soulless zombies. That's when I looked closer and my heart dropped. They were MP citizens, my citizens. Yet their color appeared to be drained. Then it had hit me. These were some of my soldiers that had died during the many battles we've had in the MP. Xercus was country of the Dead and other creature, such as hobgoblins, warlocks, and so on. If you were as dreadful as Satan on Earth, you'd land up in Xercus when you die. But when soldiers died from the MP, they are sent to Xercus, to beg mercy from Aries. I continued to look out the window and saw an enormous castle, all black as if it were burned down and reconstructed.

Bonzai looked at me and whispered in my ear. "I know it's a dump, but we have good beds." He paused. "But I suggest to you to *never* try whatever Aries cooks. It's completely horrid!" He started making gagging gestures.

I giggled and smiled. I thought I would never smile at Xercus, but things happen and God is one crazy dude. We got closer to the castle and parked in the front. Aries got out first and his two sons as well.

When I started to open my door, Bonzai appeared and opened it for me. "After you, my lady." He gave me his hand.

"Thank you, Bonzai," I said, taking his hand, and got out of the SUV. The air smelled like dirt and decay. The castle was bigger on the inside than it looked on the outside. I felt so tiny and weak. As the guards took my bags, I felt the eyes of the servants on me. I turned to look at their crowd. There were more than fifty of them! I looked back at Aries and he nodded at me as if to say, *Don't be shy, go ahead.* I looked back to the crowd and felt all of my courage melt away.

That's when I felt someone take my left hand. I turned to see who had. I was staring into Bonzai's kind green eyes. He smiled. "Don't worry. I've got you covered." He winked and then turned to address the crowd of servants. "This is Princess Kyra Rumblen Count, from the MP. She will be staying with us for a while. I expect everyone to treat her like royalty – "

"Oh, no! I'm okay with whatever you guys want to treat me," I interrupted. "I just want to say . . . um . . ." My mind went blank. I should have just kept my mouth shut. I looked at Bonzai and saw that he was trying to hide his smile and that he was trying not to laugh.

He quickly recovered and continued to talk. "All right, where's Darq?"

A girl stepped to the front of the crowd. She had beautiful wavy dark brown hair and was as white as snow. Her eyes were a faded hazel, and she seemed to be 118 as well. She was skinny and wore a maid suit. Her nametag said "Boota Betsfly." "His Highness is inside his room, painting a masterpiece." Her voice was fragile as if she were about to break down. She looked everywhere except at me.

"Thank you. The rest of you should get back to work and tell the chef to prepare a good meal for breakfast."

The crowd quickly got back to work. Bonzai turned to me. "I can tell that you're not that good at meeting new people, but that's where I come in." He looped his arm around my left arm and he turned around. Aries looked impressed while Gustav looked like he had eaten a lemon. Bonzai nodded to his stepfather. "I would like the honor to escort Ms. Count – "

"Kyra. I prefer to be called by my name. I am not any higher than you guys," I said, interrupting Bonzai again.

He looked at me and smiled. "My apologies, Kyra." He turned back to his father. "Anyways, I would like the honor of escorting Kyra to her room, if that's okay with you, Aries."

Aries nodded. "All right, but afterward, escort Kyra to Darq. He must meet her." He looked at me. "Thank you, Kyra. I will see you at breakfast." Then Aries walked into a room that was full of chatter until he went in.

Gustav looked at Bonzai and I. He growled and stomped off. When he was gone, Bonzai looked at me. "You know, most people find it rude to be interrupted while speaking, but I'm okay if you do." He smiled and led me up the stairs.

I never got to look at this place so closely. Its walls were painted a dark red color and a huge chandelier hung above the staircase. The floor was all carpet, velvet the color of red of course, and there was a homey feel. As Bonzai and I walked up the grand stairs, I was trying to think about what I am I going to do here. He led me down a long hallway, and when I was just about to ask him something, a dark figure emerged out of nowhere.

The figure spoke in a low voice. "Hello, Bonzai. I see that you have a friend."

CHAPTER 7

Darq

BONZAI GLARED AT the figure and then turned to me. "Sorry, Kyra, Darq is very – "

"Kyra?" Darq said, shocked. "This is the famous Kyra Rumblen Count everyone's been talking about? Why is she covered in dirt?"

I looked down at my shirt and saw that I looked as if I had just crawled out of a grave. Then I studied Darq. Bonzai pronounced his name as *Dar*, hinting that the *q* in Darq was silent. He appeared to be older than Bonzai, Gustav, and I, probably by a few years. He had short dark blond hair that was just one shade away from being blond, and yet, he had small traces of brown strands in his hair. He appeared strong and he had a body of a salsa dancer. He had his father's face and his eyes were dark gray, not Luna's eyes or Aries's eyes though. He had paint on his hands and was wearing a T-shirt and dark blue jeans that laid low on his hips. I noticed that his feet were bare and that he wasn't wearing shoes. And he thought that he had the right to comment about me being . . . well, *normal.* I smiled at him, tightly. "So you're Darq. You're the reason Gustav almost killed me." I paused. "And by the way, at least I'm wearing shoes."

He was startled about how forward I was, but a lot of people are surprised by my forwardness. Then he turned to his brother. "Dude, she's cute." He eyed me head to toe. "Not hot, but she's like super cute. I'll see you at breakfast." He nodded at me and disappeared through a door.

Bonzai turned to me and sighed. "Well, this wasn't the best introduction, was it?"

I smiled. "Sorry. Princesses only lie once a week."

He smiled and started walking. I jogged to catch up. The hallway had many doors, and the walls were ivy green. We finally stopped in front of a door at the end of the hallway and Bonzai took something out of his jeans pocket. It was a key marked "Kyra." He put the key in the lock and twisted it until we heard a snap. Then he turned to me. "Okay, Kyra. This is your new room." Finally he opened the door.

I was astonished. The room was huge, similar to my room in the MP, but bigger. It had a chandelier in the center, dark red walls and dark hard wood flooring. I looked around in awe. "Wow. This is so . . . big." There was plasma TV on the left wall, and lava lamps lighted up the room. There was a door leading to my own personal bathroom that looked hard to operate, a queen-sized bed that had soft silk covers with a canopy on top of it, a vanity mirror with all sorts of makeup, creams, and perfumes I have never seen before, and drawers that were more than enough to put all of my things in it. I turned toward Bonzai. "This is *my* room? It's so grand." I paused. "Are you sure I'm worth all of this?" I gestured all of the room.

Bonzai looked shocked. "Why would you ask that? You're possibly the only girl, besides Boota who's Darq's servant, that's been in the castle since – " He paused, but I knew what he was going to say: since Luna died. His eyes were a sad green now, losing its shine. We were both silent. Finally, he let out a shaky sigh and sat down on my bed. "Have you ever felt like starting over? If I could change one thing that happened, I would change that battle. I would make sure my mother had nothing to do with that war." His voice was shaky and he turned away from me. At first, it looked like he was just looking at the scene behind the curtains, but then I saw his shoulders shaking.

"Oh, Bonzai." I went over to him and put my hand on his shoulders. "Don't cry. Your mother would be proud of you and don't you think she can't see what a lovely man you are. You're kind, loving an – "

He moved like lightning. He turned around and embraced me in a long hug. His body felt warm against mine and I gasped at his strength. He was trying to be gentle, but I hug him tightly and stroked his head. I didn't know what to do at the time. He quickly drew away, wiping his tears. "Sorry. I don't know what came over me. I just need a hug and you remind me so much of my mother." He sniffed and reached for a napkin from inside the drawer next to the bed. He blew his nose and looked at me. "You know, I've never cried after what happened to her. I thought I got over it already, but sometimes love that strong can't be broken." He looked sad, like a puppy with no bone.

"I know what it's like to lose someone you love. I lost my family in the same battle and I had to become full princess of the MP. It was your mother that taught me how to be rule and without her teaching me before, I wouldn't be the woman

I am today." I smiled, sadly, at him and put my arm around him. It seemed like a good thing to do.

Bonzai got up and headed to the door, them he stopped. He looked back at me. "Thank you again, Kyra. I'll be on the other side of the hall if you need me, okay?"

I nodded and he went out the door, leaving the door open. I took a look at the clock. It read 5:00 a.m. I sighed. Only four hours of sleep. I didn't even change out of my tee and I went under the silk covers. It felt soft like home. *This is my home now*, I reminded myself. It took a while for sleep to pull me under, but it did eventually. And I dreamt of home with my family alive.

CHAPTER 8

First Impression

I WAS SLEEPING until I felt a presence in the room. I heard heavy footsteps, too heavy to be a girl. I realized it might have been an intruder. That's when I shot up, bumping my head against Aries. "Ouch!" I complained, as I glared at Aries, who was rubbing his forehead. "Why were you so close to my face?"

"Sorry. I walked in and saw that you weren't breathing! I was about to see if your heart was beating, but that's when you woke up," He then stared at me. "Why weren't you breathing?"

"That's how vamps sleep! We don't breathe! Ever heard of the saying 'I slept like the dead'?" I exclaimed. I looked around at the room. It was lit up by the light outside and seemed homier than last night. The events that happened yesterday swarmed back into my head and I realized I was in my room in the Xercus Castle.

Aries groaned. "Well, sorry! Last time I checked I'm *not* a vamp!" He paused. "By the way, it's 9:00am and breakfast is in thirty minutes! So hurry up! When the boys are hungry, they tend to rip each other apart. No pressure." He turned and walked out of the room, his footsteps echoed throughout the hallway. I got up and closed the door. Then I got my toothbrush and toothpaste out of my luggage and went to the bathroom to take a shower. Sure enough, there was hot water and cold water and tulip-scented shampoo and conditioner. I took a shower and wrapped a towel around my body and hair. The towels felt soft and wrapped around me perfectly. I brushed my teeth and got out of the washroom. I was about to open my luggage to pick a dress, when I saw a note.

It said, *Kyra, I would like you to wear Luna's favorite dress. She would have liked you to be wearing it for this occasion. See you at the table! – Aries.*

I looked at my bed. Sitting there was a short strapless dress that went up to my knees. It was a dark purple, made out of velvet, with a purple flower on the waist. I slipped it on, and surprisingly, it fitted like it was made for me. I went to the mirror and did a double take. The dress showed off my curves and I look exactly like Luna. I dried my hair, applied eyeliner, add some cream to define my curls, and straightened my bangs. I put on a headband that had a purple flower on it and purple earrings with a bat necklace. I examined my work and stepped back, impressed. Finally, I sprayed on perfume and slipped on purple high heels. I took my room key and headed out the door. As I walked to the dining hall, several servants looked at me and whispered to one another, *Isn't that Kyra Rumblen Count? Or is Queen Luna back from the grave?* When I reached the doors to the hall, I held my head high with confidence and push open the doors.

I did not expect to see Aries, Darq, Gustav, and Bonzai fighting, that's for sure. Aries was yelling at the boys to stop, Darq was throwing glass at the wall and Gustav and Bonzai were rolling on the floor throwing punches at each other. I was definitely late by a minute. I stared at the scene, realizing I should have taken Aries warning about the boys seriously. I knew that if I didn't stop this fight, someone would definitely get hurt. I stood on top of an empty table, making sure my dress didn't come up, and put two fingers to my lips and let out a high pitch whistle. Aries stopped yelling to stare at me, his mouth opened as if he didn't know what to say. Darq looked me, amazed, while Bonzai and Gustav stared up at me, shocked and confused. I cleared my throat. "It appears that you boys are hungry," I glared at them all, trying to look as cold as possible and as mature as Luna. "But that gives you all no reason to act like foolish hobgoblins!" I rubbed my temple. Then I gestured to Bonzai and Gustav. "You two get off of the floor and sit at the table. Right. Now." To my surprise, they got up quickly and walked quickly to the table. I looked at Darq and sighed. "You know, just because you have nothing to do, that doesn't mean you can break everything! Go fetch somebody to clean up this mess and get us new plates." He ran out the door without any hesitation. Finally, I turned to my father-in-law and grinned. "Now that's how you take care of boys."

He stared at me in awe. "You look just like Luna. You got the hair, the beauty, the clothes, personality, and you know just what to do," his eyes widened. "Should I sit down?"

"It would be nice if you help me down from this table!" I exclaimed to him. He came over and gave me his hand. I jumped down and thanked him. Then I headed to the table and sat down next to Gustav, in front of Bonzai. Both boys stared at me, shocked, as I sat. I glared at both of them. "You know, staring is impolite." That stopped both of them. They looked down at their hands until Darq returned with Boota trailing behind him, juggling a stack of plates. I ran to her side and took half of the plates from her, and when she tried to protest, I hushed her. Everybody stared at me as I carried the plates and handed them out. Darq, Bonzai, and Aries thanked me as I handed them the plates, but Gustav just looked at me, gave me a dirty look, as he took the plate. I sighed with both relief and disappointment. As much as I could impress everybody else, I knew I needed a good impression from Gustav because, in reality, I don't need an enemy.

CHAPTER 9

Another Side of Darq

AFTER EATING A full plate of eggs, bacon, toast, and a cup of orange juice, I looked at the men in front of me, who are silently eating, not saying a word. "So how's everyone's day so far?" I cursed myself for being so awkward. Silence pierced the room. Even the servants waiting next to the doors said nothing. I waited for a minute and then sighed. "You guys are strangely quiet. Did something happen?"

Gustav was the first to talk. "Yes, something did happen." He glared at me with disgust. "You came here." He quickly pushed back his chair and made for the exit, but then halted. He turned to his father. "Excuse me, but I think that I'm going to go the weapons room to train." He faced away and kicked open the doors and disappeared into the hallway, leaving us all stunned.

Aries sighed as he wiped his mouth with a pearl white napkin. "I am so sor – "

"You really need to stop apologizing for Gustav. It's not your fault that he hates me. He thinks that I have something to do with Luna's death." I paused. "And he's right."

Bonzai stopped eating and looked at me with complete rage. "For the love of God! Stop it, stop it right now, Kyra. You had nothing to do with her death and I cannot just sit here, hearing you say bad things about yourself!" He stood up, knocking down his chair, and stomped out of the room.

Darq sighed. "And then, there were three."

Aries glared at him and got to his feet. "Please excuse me, but I have to deal with two young men." He looked at me. "You looked ravishing today. If you want, you can go – "

I didn't let him finish his sentence. I ran. I ran out of the room, nearly knocking over Boota. I mumbled an apology and ran to my room, high heels in my hand. I didn't stop running until I got to my room. I fumbled with my keys and finally pushed it into the lock and threw open the door. I closed it and pressed my back against the door. I sat down and felt hot tears running down my cheek. I sat there, crying my heart out and then I stood, wiping my tears. I went into the bathroom and washed my face. After drying, I took the dress off carefully and threw on sweatpants and a dark blue tank top. Then, I started to unpack. I put away all of my clothes in the drawers and my vanity things on a table. After, I opened my duffel bag that held all of my precious items from home. I inspected everything, making sure they were all in perfect conditions, and then I felt tears slowly crawl down my face as I looked at my fallen star. It was a gift from Luna, her gift to me the day before the war. She told me that she saw it fall out of the sky and went to find it. When she found it, she clutched it in her hands and ran to my castle. I was on the steps, wondering what I'll do during the war when she came. I looked at her, then the star, and then back to her. I hugged her and took the star and kept it in my soul bag. I still have it, in remembrance of a loyal friend. I closed my eyes and clutch the star close to my chest; tears welled up in my eyes.

"Are you okay?"

I jumped to my feet, the star in my hand, fangs bared.

Darq stood at the doorway, hands on his hips, looking at me with a curious expression. "Can I come in? Or will you bite my neck?"

I quickly calmed down and felt my teeth slit back to normal. "Come on in." I placed the star gently inside my bag and closed the zipper. I looked at him. He was wearing the same blue striped shirt and low-hanging jeans that he wore at breakfast.

He walked over to where I was sitting on the floor and sat down. "Listen. I know Gustav can be a little rude – "

"A little? More like a lot!"

"Listen. He can be a little rude, but that's because of our mom's death. He loved her so much that, when she was killed, he swore on the angels that he would get revenge, and since you are connected to the war, he thinks that he can torture you." He placed an arm around my shoulders. "But you have something that you can use against him."

"Really? And what's that?" I asked him sarcastically.

"Your looks and personality. You stopped him from killing Bonzai before breakfast! No one has ever stopped Gustav when he's fighting! You look so much like our mom, and if you can convince him that you loved her as much as he did – "

"I did love her as much as he did! She was my mentor! My best friend! She was like another mother to me! She shouldn't have died! I should have just sworn my oath to Aries! Then this war wouldn't have started!" I started to cry again, the tears streaming down my cheeks.

"Oh no, don't do that," Darq said softy, as he wrapped me in his arms. I felt so safe, and for some reason, I felt his heart beat in time with my heart. I looked up at his face. His dark gray eyes showed protectiveness and he looked at me with love. "You're the reason we're actually not tearing each other apart. You're beautiful and I know that you'll be a wonderful queen of Xercus and the MP."

I sniffed. "You really think so?"

"I know so."

"But – "

I stopped when he pulled me into a kiss. I felt a rush of adrenaline and without thinking I deepened the kiss. I ran my fingers through his silky hair, pulling him closer. He responded by holding my cheeks with his hands, his delicate fingers caressing my cheek, and pressing his body against mine. His kisses were hard and sloppy, and it was easy to tell he wasn't sure how to kiss. It was a nice kiss that held meaning, and though something felt out of place, we ignored it. Still, I didn't quite feel a spark; it was more like a sympathy kiss. Then, without even knowing, we ended up with him on top of me, on the floor. We were so distracted; we didn't hear the door burst open right away.

CHAPTER 10

An Unexpected Guest

WE BOTH JUMPED to our feet. Darq jumped in front of me, as I pulled out my dagger from my bag. I pushed Darq out of the way and threw the dagger at the figure, which was at the door. The figure swung into the room, dodging the dagger, and into the light. That's when I saw her face. "Angela? Angela Scarblood?" I said, shocked.

"Well, who did you think it was?" she answered. Angela looked exactly the way as she did four years ago; of course she rarely aged in looks. She was the same age as me, with short curly brown hair. She was taller than me and had curvy body. Her eyes were ivy green and her skin was one shade darker than mine. She looked at me with the same arrogant expression. She was grinning. "Damn girl! You haven't age at all! What kind of face cream are you using? And what do we have here?" Her eyes landed on Darq, who was confused. "Making out with a pretty boy, are we?" She raised her eyebrows.

I glared at my friend. "This is Darq Deatheye. I'm here because – "

"I already know! I'm here to warn you." Her sly expression slipped away and was replaced with a dead serious look. "Word has it that someone's planning on creating another battle, this time the kingdoms against an army of demons."

I was shocked. "No. That can't be." I looked at Darq. "Do you know anything about this?"

He was shaking his head. "I had no idea. I don't even know who this girl is!"

Angela grinned at him. "Clueless and hot. I like them like that. I'm Angela Scarblood, Angel of Death. But you can call me Angel, though I don't act like one." She winked at him and Darq paled even more.

I groaned. "I'll explain later," I said to Darq. I looked back at Angela. "Do you know who is creating this battle?"

"Someone powerful. Guess?"

I gave her a look instead.

Her expression turned more serious. "A hybrid, like you and as powerful as you are. That's all I know."

"Can't you stop him or her?"

"Um, hello. I'm a death angel, not a peace-making death angel."

Angela was one of the most powerful death angels I knew. She could kill someone on the spot whenever she wanted to, only if they aren't as powerful as a hybrid. But she was also able to revive any pure soul back to life. She was powerful but she was very clumsy. Yet when you needed her, she was always there.

I looked at Darq. "We need to tell Aries."

He frowned. "He's in a meeting – "

I didn't wait. I ran out of the room, with Darq and Angela right behind me. I passed several rooms, and without thinking, I jumped from the top of the stairs. I heard Angela scream and Darq shout when they saw what I had done, but I landed gracefully on all fours. I jumped up, dashed through the east wings and threw open the doors leading into the meeting room, which had dark blue walls and mahogany wood flooring. Inside the room was a long table with several people sitting there. They all looked at me and stared and I realized that I was wearing just a tank top and sweatpants, and I looked exactly like Luna. They all started to whisper to each other, *Oh my god, Luna's back. Who is that? Queen Luna is back to haunt us! Wait, is that Queen Luna?* Sitting at the head seat was Aries, dressed in a black business suit with a navy blue tie. He stared at me with confusion. "Kyra – ," he began to say. Hearing my name, some of the people at the table relaxed while others shot me a dirty, yet horrified, look.

"We have a problem. Like, a *big* problem," I interrupted him, my tone dead serious. I walked over to him and turned to address the group of people. "Someone's trying to create another battle. If any of you know anything about this, please raise your hand."

No one raised their hand and silence pierced the room, as I saw that my answer was a chorus of horrified faces peering at me. Aries looked at me with a shocked look. "What do you mean, Kyra?"

I looked at him. "Someone doesn't like the idea of there being peace between our countries! A hybrid is trying to put us into a blood-pouring battle! We need to find out who is this person and how we can stop him or her!"

"Why should we help you?" someone said.

“Your warriors almost slaughtered our nation!” another person yelled.

Aries cleared his voice. “Everyone, be quiet! Kyra is here to help us. She will be marrying one of my sons.” Everyone gasped.

I looked at them with an icy look. “We need a plan. For now, I want everybody to calm down and report to Aries and I if you find any useful clues. That is all for now.” I turned and walked out of the room, leaving them all staring at the door.

CHAPTER II

How the Deatheye Boys Were Created

I FOUND ANGELA and Darq waiting for me outside of the meeting room, both panting and doubled over. "Next time . . . wait for us." Angela gasped, trying to catch her breath. "I never thought that you would actually jump off the very top of the stairs."

I shrugged. "I learnt that from my mom. All you have to do is think that you're the lightest person in the world and there you go." I looked at Darq who was still doubled over. "Are you all right?"

He managed to raise his head. "I'm not that good at running. I'm Fey, so we can't run without getting drained."

Angela stared at him, suddenly okay and fascinated. "You're fey? As in a faery?" She giggled. "Wow, you seem too macho to be a flying pest. Then again, you aren't so strongly built . . . I've never met a male fey before."

Darq shot her a glare. "Well, guess what? That rumor that we can fly only goes for the girl fey clan! I'm part of the boy fey clan and we can only talk to animals."

I realized something. "Wait a minute. If you're fey and Bonzai's a vamp . . . then what is Gustav?" I never really thought about it, but I realized that they all were different creatures.

Darq looked at me with an uncertain look. "Do you really want to know?"

I nodded.

He sighed. "Gustav is a dark angel."

Angela gaped and then looked confused. "There's no way you have dark angel blood in your family's bloodline. Aries is a warrior god and Luna was a vamp. Either of them didn't possess such unearthly powers. You need to have one evil parent and one angel parent. Like me, except I'm a death angel because I had a dark angel mom and an evil dad."

I gasped, my eyes widening as I still registered what Darq had said. "What? It doesn't make sense. Like Angela just said, Aries is one of the most powerful war gods and Luna was a vamp. But I don't get how you're fey, Bonzai's just a vamp, and Gustav is a damn dark angel!"

He finally recovered from the run and sat on the floor, as if he were going to launch into a huge story. "I came from different mother. I was the first child and my mother was the fey queen, Gabby Flystar. My mother wanted a girl and she disowned me when I was born. I'm Aries's son, not hers. So, she left us after I was born. After a few years, my father met Luna Fairwind, who was leader of the Xercus vamp clan. My father fell in love with her in an instant. They got married and had Gustav. But something went wrong. A female death angel was in love with Aries and got mad when she realized he loved Luna. So she cursed Luna. The curse was '*for the first born shall not be a joy, but a burden that will cause havoc among every soul unless true love is found.*' When Gustav was born, Luna and Aries were shocked. Their first child had blue eyes, blue eyes that could cause pain, even death when wanted. He didn't cry when he came, because he was dead. He has no heartbeat. He is cursed and he seeks pleasure through pain. Luna was terrified of Gustav but Aries looked at him and said, 'He's our child, and we are his parents.' Gustav grew up to be our father's dream son come true. He is a professional swordsman and knows every striking part of the body. But his powers are scary. I remember playing goldfish with him when he was seven years old and I was twelve years old and I had won. He got mad and before I could cool him down, he had me clutching my stomach in agony. He just sat there, grinning, laughing at me. The pain was horrible and I felt like I was going to die and I was about to. But then our father burst into the room and knocked over Gustav. That's when I was able to breathe. He's powerful and he can kill anything. After a month, Bonzai was born. A love angel blessed him because the angel saw what had happened to Gustav, so he was born as a love angel, to create balance. All was well and we were all happy, except for Gustav of course. But when Bonzai was ten, a rogue vamp bit him. Our father and Luna buried him in the backyard that day. But they didn't know that he got turned. They thought the vamp drained him. One night, after a few years, Luna was beside the grave, mourning over him. She was shocked when his hand emerged out of the dirt, reaching for life." Darq's voice shook. "She yelled for our father as she dug him out. By the time Aries and I got to her, she was crying. He wasn't strong enough to dig himself out of the grave. When we got him out, he was weak. I stared at him and felt a pang of hope. I realized the only way to save him was to give him some blood. I was about to let him drink my blood, but Luna was already feeding him her blood from her wrist, urging him to drink his full. After a few gulps, he opened his eyes. They were emerald green, not his old dark gray eyes. He gasped for air and jumped to his feet. He looked at me and smiled. 'Hi, big bro,' he said to me, and I hugged him. He was cold to the touch and covered in dirt, but I didn't care. He was alive, and that's what mattered. Then he pulled away, looked at Aries and his smile was replaced with a frown. 'Who are you?' he asked. Our father was hurt. He started to freak out, telling Bonzai that he was his father, but Bonzai frowned and simply said that he was wrong. He still thinks that Aries isn't his father but he calls him his stepfather or Aries. It kills Aries every day, knowing that his youngest son will never call him father again."

We were all silent. Then Angela broke the silence. "Wow. That is one sad story." She wiped away tears that managed to slip out. "I can't believe all of this happened to you guys."

Darq looked at her, with a sad look. "I can't believe it either."

CHAPTER 12

The Unexpected

DARQ, ANGELA, AND I went our ways: Darq to his room, Angela out to find a room, and myself, to my room. I called Boota and told her to bring my lunch and dinner up to my room, whenever she wanted. I didn't think I could survive another fight with Gustav. I went into my room, closed the door behind me and collapsed onto the bed. I fell into a deep sleep, with no dreams and no nightmares.

* * *

I woke up the next day and went straight to the bathroom, ignoring everything else. After emerging from the bathroom, still in the clothes I wore the day before, I walked blindly to my mirror and untied my hair, letting it flow down my back.

When I looked at the mirror, I felt a scream reach my throat, but no sound came out. Sitting at the foot of my bed was Gustav, who was looking at me with a look I have never seen him give me. It looked like a look of hunger, as if he wanted something, as if he needed something. I whirled around to face him. "Gustav! You scared me half to death! How did you get in?" I steadied a hand on the wall, not trusting my legs that felt like jelly, and I had a hand over my heart, as if trying to calm it down.

He took in my clothing and got off the bed. “I stole Boota’s key. I had to see you.” He looked impatient.

“What is it?” I asked.

“Come closer,” he said, with a seductive voice.

“What?” I was shocked. He had never asked me to come to him. In fact, he never even said anything to me except for rude things.

“You heard me. Come closer.” He grinned. “Unless you’re afraid.”

I hated being challenge. I walked toward him until I was so close to him, our bodies touched. A rush of electricity surged through me. I looked up into his blue eyes and I knew he had felt it too. “What is it?” I asked again, with a hint of impatience.

“I assume that Darq told you all about us, hasn’t he? Well, then you know that I’m a dark angel.” His blue eyes twinkled wickedly, sending shivers up my back. “Today’s the day I was cursed. Every year, my mother would always cheer me up on this day, but she can’t anymore. So I really need to be distracted right now.” He sighed. “Well, here goes nothing.”

Before I could stop him or even react, he grabbed both of my arms and kissed me on the lips. His kisses were hard and hungry, demanding more. I went numb in his arms and felt my hands run through his hair. I knew I should’ve stop. It wasn’t right. He hated me. He blamed me for what happened to Luna. But my body wasn’t listening. “The bed,” he muttered between kisses. I gasped in surprise as he swept me off my feet and carried me to the bed. He gently dropped me on the bed, my head on a pillow. I was breathing hard. He climbed onto the bed and aligned his body onto mine, making sure not to crush me. He rested his elbows on either side on my head and looked down on me with wide eyes. I stared up at him, wondering how did this happen. I raised my hand and touched his face gently but cautiously in case he was about to go back to cold old Gustav. “Why did you act as if you hated me the second you saw me?”

He looked down on me and slowly lowered his face until our noses were touching. He smelled like fresh minty soap and citrus shampoo. “I wasn’t thinking. You look so much like my mother, and she hated me. But whenever my curse day comes, she suddenly changes and comforts me with love and kindness. But when she died “ – he paused – ” I felt my world crash down. I felt like garbage. I had no one to cheer me up when I was sad and no one to give me the love my mom used to. So when I saw you, I knew that you would be a replica of my mother. So I decided to hate you, so you would stay away from me. But that didn’t go well. When you came for breakfast and actually stopped us from wrecking the place, I was shocked and impressed. You sound like Luna and you looked more like her in that dress. After I stomped off, I realized that I couldn’t hate you because no one can hate you without dying on the inside.” He pressed his body against mine, our thighs flushed together, his fingers trailing through my hair.

I put my arms to my sides and stared into his blue eyes that had darkened. "Well, what do you want to do now?" My voice shook as I spoke.

He grinned down at me. "I want to do this." He leaned closer until our lips touched. He went soft, trying to control himself. I immediately went limp under him, letting him pleasure himself. And surprisingly, I kissed him back with more force. He deepened the kiss, his mouth pressing harder down on mine, and just like that, a spark flicked in between us and he felt it as well. He stroked my arms hard and lovingly while I pulled him closer, allowing him to break the little gap we had separating us and I felt him put his hands on my thigh, travelling up in the direction I wasn't hoping he'd travel. I felt a rush of hunger and confusion come over me and I realized that I needed to stop what was happening before we took it too far. So without thinking, I bit his lip, hard. He gasped in surprise, possibly in pain as well, and I took the opportunity to shove him off me. He went flying off the bed, onto the floor. I jumped off the bed. Gustav was on his feet already, looking at me with confusion and frustration. "Why did you do that?" he demanded, his voice strong but his hands were shaking.

There was blood on his lips, and then I realized that my fangs must have came out. My fangs slit back into my mouth and I looked at him from a different perspective. His hair was all ruffled and his eyes were a hurt, stormy blue. "I-I can't do this," I stammered. "I'm not ready to go that far. Plus it won't be fair to your brothers."

Gustav swore under his breath and raked a hand through his hair. "I'm sorry. I felt a spark between us. Didn't you? Please tell me you felt it? I did. What do you think?" He looked at me, his eyes pleading.

I looked away, unable to lie to his face. "I think you should get out. Right now."

Gustav looked at me, with a hurt expression, and then he vanished through the door, leaving me to wonder what have I done now.

CHAPTER 13

Training

AFTER SOBBING OUT of frustration into a pillow, I decided that I had to stay on top of things. Not only did I have to worry about my love life but I also had to deal with a new upcoming battle. I looked down at my luggage. I mostly packed dresses, thinking that I just had to be formal, but in my secret luggage pocket, I packed my fighting and training gear just in case I needed it. It was a black leather vest, black leather tights, and black combat boots that allowed me to move freely. I also had battle gear in case of a battle situation. I would have worn my black leather jacket, but I decided not to. I slipped them on and attached my belt that was able to hold a lot of weapons. I tied my hair into a high tight ponytail, got my daggers, knives, and sword, and placed them into the slots on my belt. I stood in front of the mirror, examining my work. I looked tough and exactly like Luna on the day of the war that ended her life. Though she didn't exactly look really tough because she was kind hearted. I on the other hand looked ready to kill. That's how I like to look. I got my room key and closed the door behind me. As I walked down the hallway, all of the servants did a double take when they saw me. I walked with my head up, ignoring their stares. I decided that I needed to test my skill, and instead of running down the stairs, I jumped from the top and landed on my feet without making any sound. I ran swiftly down the east hallway, only stopping at the door of the personal training room that was only for Aries and his family. I held my breath and opened the door a little. No one was in there. I opened the door a little more and slipped in, making sure no one saw me enter. I gazed around the room. It was massive and had black walls with hard wood flooring. There were bright lights that burned my eyes as I stared at the weapons. There were swords of all kinds, daggers, bows and arrows, and guns. It was strange to see guns there: they weren't happy about using them, mostly for shoot offs. There were targets and punching bags. Ignoring the other weapons, I pulled out one of my daggers and threw it at one of the targets. It had hit home. I grinned. *I guess I'm not that rusty than I thought,* I realized, satisfied. After warming up, I began to throw daggers at the targets again and then at the dummies. When I threw all of my daggers, I turned to the dummy, my fist raised. I punched out all of my anger and kicked at the dummy, letting all of my emotions out. After thirty minutes, I was sweating and I sank to the floor. I took a break and then got back to work, taking out my crusader sword. It was once my mother's, Lilith the mother of the demons, until she gave it to me, a gift saying, *when you need the power to overcome the dark, the light will be your sword and you'll be the warrior wielding the power.* It was made out of pure silver and covered in gold. The handle was decorated with purple and pink gems. It was exactly how I wanted it to be. There was a move that I always messed up on at the MP Academy, so I practiced it. It was a challenging sword move, where you'd fake an attack to the shoulder and strike at a leg muscle, so it was a deathblow. I sucked at faking the first blow to the shoulder. Either I strike or I miss. I worked and worked but I kept messing up. I growled in frustration and threw a dagger at the target. It hit home, yet I wasn't in the mood to celebrate. Suddenly, I heard footsteps approaching the training room's door. I looked around, filled with panic, and hid in a closet, which was filled with water bottles. I huddled in the corner, listening to the sound of the door being opened and closed. Footsteps echoed through the room and I heard someone whistling. I realized it might have been Gustav, the thought causing me to huddle more into the corner. I heard a surprised gasp and realized that I left my daggers and sword in the room. I swore under my breath and waited. A minute later, I heard the room's door open and close. I let out a sigh of relief and got to my feet.

Just when I was about to open the door, the closet door flew open. Bonzai was standing there with one of my daggers in his hand, just an inch away from my throat. He gasped when he saw it was I and lowered the dagger. "God you scared me." He raked his free hand through his hair, his green eyes staring at me. "If I hadn't stopped myself from pushing the dagger into your throat, you'd be dead."

I said nothing. He was wearing black sweatpants and his usual green Nikes. His hair was ruffled, as if he had walked straight out of bed, and his green eyes twinkled. He was shirtless, showing of his broad shoulders and rippling muscles, and I urged myself not to stare. He appeared tense, as he waited for my reply. I cleared my throat. "But I'm already dead, remember?" I grinned.

He grinned and relaxed. "Well, then you'd be deader. Were you training?" He now had a curious look on his pretty face.

"Actually, I was. Until I heard someone coming, so I hid." I paused. "Who opened and closed the door?"

"I did. I came to train and I saw your daggers and sword. I realized that someone was in here, so I made heavy footsteps toward the door, opened and closed it, grabbed one of your daggers and tiptoed here to find you hiding in the closet!" He gave me a look. "You didn't have to hide. This is your home now. You can do anything you want."

I grinned. "Want to train together, then?" I asked with an amused look.

"All right, sure."

With that we got back to work. We started to stretch and then, we decided to spar with each other. In twenty seconds of fighting my hardest, Bonzai had me pinned with my back on the floor, his body over mine, his hands pinning my hands over my head. Our faces were an inch apart from each other. I was sweating, yet he appeared not winded at all. But he was breathing hard, his green eyes wide, his lips parted. Then he leaned closer to my face until our noses were touching. He stared into my eyes, and then he grinned. "Got you." Then he lowered his lips onto mine. His lips were soft, and he smelled like fresh mint soap. His hands explored my arms, as he kissed my neck. I tilted my head back, moaning, feeling him, soaked in his love, but I felt no spark. I only felt pleasure, but there wasn't a spark like I had felt with Gustav. Bonzai was soft, almost fragile, and I held back, afraid I might hurt him. Being a hybrid, any action of love became dangerous, especially when I tended to unleash my fangs without knowing. So I kept my cool, though it was hard to resist going deeper when going softer than I usually do drove me crazy. It would have been even nicer if the training room's doors weren't thrown open.

CHAPTER 14

Family Feud

BONZAI SCRAMBLED OFF me, swearing under his breath. I jumped to my feet and saw Gustav, his eyes blazing a cold blue. He was wearing the same thing he wore when he came to my room. He looked exactly like an avenging angel. Bonzai turned to look at his brother and growled. Gustav growled back, even more menacing. I stared, eyes wide, at the two. We stood there frozen, Bonzai and I, as Gustav strolled toward us. He stopped in front of his brother, his face dead serious. "How dare you? I thought that Darq would do this, but you?" he spat. "I can't believe it."

Bonzai looked as if he were going to blow up. "How dare *I?* How dare *you*! You act as if you hate Kyra, and now just because you don't like her, I can't love her? You have some nerve, angel of darkness!" he yelled, his green eyes blazed a steaming emerald.

Gustav looked him right in the eye. "I might have different feelings about her now than I did before," he said with a hard tone. He glanced at me. "Have you made your choice then? Him over me or him over me *and* Darq?"

I froze there, shocked to the core and out. *Shoot,* I thought. "Wh-what did y-you say?" I stammered.

He smiled sadly. "Your little angel friend has a big mouth. She told everybody about your little secret with Darq."

I felt dizzy as if I were going to throw up. I swore under my breath. I glared at him. "I came here to choose a spouse. Excuse me for testing the waters."

Bonzai stared at me and then at Gustav. "So. You like her now?" he asked with an uncertain tone.

"I don't like her, you fool. I love her." He was still looking at me as he said it. "I love her more than anything."

I felt like someone had just punched me right in the heart, hard. *He loves me,* I thought, *Oh, lord. This isn't good.* I stared at him, horrified, and I felt butterflies fluttering in my stomach.

I was so shocked; I didn't see Bonzai run at Gustav. He knocked his brother down on his back and threw punches at him. Gustav swung up his leg, kicking Bonzai in the neck, and the two started rolling all over the floor, taking turns punching and kicking each other. I realized that if I didn't stop them, one of them would leave with a bloody nose. I pulled Gustav off Bonzai and threw him across the room. He hit the wall and slumped to the floor. I looked down at Bonzai. He got up and I saw that he got scratched on his chest and that his lip was bleeding. He looked at me. "Don't follow me and don't *ever* talk to me. Is that clear?" he told me in a harsh, shaky voice and he didn't wait for my response. He just stomped out of the room, slamming the door. I couldn't take it; I took all of my daggers, knives, and my sword and ran out of the room, crying. I didn't stop until I got to my door. I fumbled with the key and finally pushed open the door and slammed it shut. I threw myself onto the bed, sobbing for a good five minutes. *It's the third day and I'm already crying,* I thought. *God, I hate love.* I slept in my gear, dreaming about a sky full of falling stars.

* * *

I woke up the next day with kinks in my neck. I saw that there was a note on my dresser. I got up and snatched it. I read it, *Kyra, I'm sorry but there won't be any breakfast. I'm going to be at a meeting about this "upcoming battle" and I should be back by midnight. Boota will be there with your breakfast and I'm sorry about what happened with you and the boys . . . Gustav told me what happened and I know that you will make the right choice. You may want to talk to them. But don't stress about this. In the afternoon, the castle is throwing a welcome party to Siddiqis Starburn. I know he's one of your best friends! Go and enjoy it! – Aries*

I stood there for a second and then I heard a knock at the door. I opened it to find Boota, holding a tray full of food. She said a quiet good morning and rushed to the bed, to put down the tray. Then she walked to the door and was about to leave until she saw my face. I had dark circles under my red eye, a bunch of tearstains, and my fangs were peeking out because depression brought them fully out and sometimes I couldn't even control them. In short form, I looked like a hot mess with fangs. "Oh god. Are you all right, Ms. Count?" she asked with a worried expression as she shut the door.

"Please call me Kyra, Boota. Come sit on the bed with me. I need a girl to talk to," I told her, ignoring the fact she was Darq's servant.

She looked uncertain. "His Highness would punish me, Ms. Count. I don't know."

"I order you to stop calling me Ms. Count and call me Kyra and I order you to sit down with me on the bed." I knew that by ordering her, she would have to do it.

She sighed, giving up. We walked to the bed and sat down. She carefully sat on the edge while I leaned back against the pillows. I looked at her. She was wearing a maid outfit that really didn't suit her. Her hair was tied in a tight bun and her hazel eyes looking down at the floor.

I sighed. "I hate love." My fangs finally slit back into my mouth and my teeth went back to normal.

Boota looked at me with a confused look. "How come?"

I smiled sadly. "If you had two boys fighting over you, you'd understand."

She nodded and silence was exchanged.

Then, I looked at her with a curious look. "Why are you a maid?"

She looked at me, startled. "I beg your pardon?"

"It's just you're so young. Most maids are about 350!"

"I was born in a poor family," she explained. "My father's the cook and my mum is Lord Aries's maid. My family lived here before the Artistic Darq was born – "

"*The Artistic Darq*?" I laughed.

She smiled. "He's the best painter. He can paint anything. That's why we call him the Artistic Darq. Anyways back to your question. My family lived here since the Artistic Darq was born, and when he needed a maid, I was hired. I live in the servant quarters. As long as I have the blood of a Betsfly, I'm destined to be a maid. It's in my blood."

"That's not in your blood! You're a ravishing young lady!" I exclaimed. I paused. "You never told me what you are."

She smiled shyly. "I'm half vamp, half hobgoblin. My mom's a vamp and my dad's a hobgoblin."

I gawked. "What? You're telling me that you're part hobgoblin? I get the whole vamp part, though you act nothing like one, but hobgoblin? I've met many hobgoblins and let me tell you something. They are not as polite as you are!"

She giggled. "I'm more vamp than hobgoblin. I have a stronger vamp bloodline than hobgoblin." She then went serious. "Am I actually pretty?"

I gave her a look of complete disbelief. "I can't believe you just asked that! You shouldn't be working as a maid! You look like a girl from the girl fey clan! We need to show people that." I suddenly got an idea. I jumped off the bed and ran to the wardrobe full of dresses that I had never seen before. I pulled it open and inspected the dresses. I picked two party dresses and laid them next to Boota. I placed my hands on my hips, grinning, staring down at a very confused Boota. "My dear," I said with an amusing voice, "time to have a little fun."

CHAPTER 15

Let's Party

AFTER USING THE bathroom and eating breakfast, I ushered Boota into the bathroom, with a dress in her hand. She protested, but as soon as I ordered her, she stomped into the washroom, muttering under her breath. I went to my changing room, my dress in tow. I emerged in it, after a minute, before Boota. After three minutes, she finally came out with her dress on. She looked nervous. "How do I look?"

I stared at her and grinned with victory. I knew that dress was perfect for her; it fit her just enough to show off her figure. It was a strapless dark evergreen dress that went up to her knees, exposing her beautiful legs and it brought out her hazel eyes. "You look awesome!" I squealed with pure delight. "I knew this would be perfect! What about me?" I posed for her.

She laughed, her hazel eyes bright. "You look amazing!"

I smoothed out my dress. It was a strapless midnight blue that stopped above my knees, showing off a little bit of my thighs. I was so relieved to see that Boota shaved her legs or else we may have been in a tough situation. Since it was the morning, I decided to keep both dresses simple yet cute. I made Boota sit in the chair in front of my mirror, which was loaded with makeup. I applied eyeliner on her, then on myself, only on the bottom of course, and a little blush on both of us. Then, to top it all off, I applied dark sexy pink color lipstick with clear lip-gloss, and I used a soft pink lip-gloss for Boota.

Finally, we stood side-by-side in front of the mirror. I felt victory wash over me, and when I saw Boota's expression, I laughed. "I see you have no idea what eyeliner, a little blush, and lip-gloss could do to you."

She stared at her reflection, stunned. "I-I can't believe this is me. It's like a fairytale." She turned to me and hugged me. I hugged her back. "Thank you, Kyra," Boota mumbled through the hug.

"Don't thank me. I just showed you how pretty you really are," I said, smiling.

She pulled away and smiled. "So what do we do now?"

I grinned, deviously. "My old friend from MP Academy, Siddiqis Starburn, is coming to the castle and the castle's throwing him an afternoon welcome party. I say we go crash it."

Boota's eyes widened. "Siddiqis Starburn? *The Siddiqis Starburn?* Isn't he, like, the hottie that has a bad boy charm?"

I chuckled. "Yep, that's him."

She looked as if she were going to faint. "I can't believe I'm going to meet him!" Then, her face dropped. "But I can't go."

"What do you mean?" I asked, spraying perfume on both of us.

She coughed at the perfume. "I'm Lord Darq's servant. The party's only for royalty and friends of royalty!" she said with a sad voice.

I grinned. "You may be Darq's servant, but you're also my friend, and I happen to be royalty."

She looked at me with wide unbelieving eyes, and then she squealed with delight. "Thank you so – "

"Stop saying thank you so we could actually go."

She nodded. Then I grabbed my clutch, dropped my room key inside it, and we were out the door. As we walked to the party hall, several servants gawked at Boota, and when one female servant gave her a dirty look, I shot the girl a glare that took the color out of her.

When we got to the hall's entrance, Boota stiffened and I knew why. There was a huge line of people, all of the females were dressed in dresses that were too elegant and all of the males were wearing tuxedos. There was a tall muscled man in the front, the bouncer, who was holding the VIP list, making sure the woman in front of him was allowed in. Boota's eyes widened. "Kyra, are you sure about this? Even if we manage to get to the front, I'm not even on the VIP list!"

"Don't worry, I've got it covered!" I assured her. "What's your mom and dad's names?"

"My mom is Lady Lustra Spades of the Servic vampire clan and my dad is Sir Derek Frogstomp, head of the Xercus hobgoblins," she answered, confused on why I asked.

"Thank you. And remember, don't say a word." Then I walked up to the bouncer, ignoring the line, with Boota in tow. The people in line scowled at us, until they realized who I was and then they just stared in awe. I smiled sweetly at the bouncer, who was staring at me with a disbelieving expression. "I am Princess Kyra Rumblen Count, daughter of Curtis Count and Lilith Demonheart, and accompanying me is Ms. Boota Betsfly, daughter of Lady Lustra Spades of the Servic vampire clan and Sir Derek Frogstomp, head of the Xercus hobgoblins. I demand entry to Lord Siddiqis Starburn's welcome party." I stared at him with unblinking eyes for more effect.

The bouncer stepped aside instantly, so we could get inside. I thanked him and motioned for Boota to follow. As we entered, I took in the smell of alcohol and blood. The hall was massive and full of people. The lights were dimmed because of the vamps that weren't used to bright lights and the stereo was playing dance music. Everybody inside seemed to be talking, though there were some people who decided to dance. I looked at Boota. She had a shocked expression on her face, and I could tell she didn't expect that. I chuckled, and when we got inside, I turned to her and grinned. "So what do you think?"

Boota opened her mouth and then shut it. Her eyes widened and her gaze was on something behind me. Or someone.

Before I could turn around, I felt strong arms wrap around me from behind and a body pressed tightly against my back, embracing me into a backward bear hug. The figure holding me chuckled tauntingly in my ear. "Well, well, well. What do we have here?"

CHAPTER 16

Siddiqis

I TENSED, ABOUT to spring into action, until I realized I knew that voice. That taunting voice, those strong arms, and the way his body fit with mine like pieces in a puzzle. I relaxed. "God, Siddiqis! You scared the bats out of me!"

I didn't pull away from him; instead, I looked up to find big magenta eyes, gleaming down at me. Siddiqis grinned, showing off his perfect white teeth. "Kyra Rumblen Count. The last time I saw you was when you told me you only wanted to be friends."

I winced mentally at the painful memory. "Sorry. It wasn't working for me. We were under war. I have to put the kingdom's safety before my love life."

"We're not under war now." His eyes twinkled wickedly down at me, and I felt his stare going into my soul.

I sighed. "I'm sorry. I thought you knew. I swore to Aries that to keep peace between the kingdoms, I must marry one of his sons."

His eyes darkened for a second and then they went back to their fun magenta color. He released me and turned to Boota, who was absolutely still with shock. He smiled at her kindly. "Hello. I am not sure we have met."

She curtsied. "Hello, Lord Siddiqis Starburn. It is a pleasure to meet you. I am Boota Betsfly, servant of the Artistic Darq Deatheye."

He looked at her dress and then at her, curiously. "You don't seem to be a servant." He tilted his head as if trying to get a vibe of her.

I cleared my throat. "I decided that Boota needed a day off of work, so I brought her here." I eyed Siddiqis. "My, my. You're awfully dressed."

Siddiqis was wearing a black tuxedo and kept his hair normal. He wore expensive black shoes that were so polished they literally shined. He was a head taller than me, as usual. His dark brown hair was slightly shorter than the last time I saw him and his magenta, with a hint of hazel, eyes were still breathtaking and full of life. He was very athletic, with a lean slightly muscular body, and his slightly golden face had many girls falling. It wasn't just because he had a strong jawline or because of his mature looks. It was because of his personality. He was very cocky, and when he was in love, he was very protective. His bad-boy vibe matched his eyes and he was known as the hottest guy in the Mortal Portal. He was also a powerful hybrid, like me. He was born to shine.

He turned back to me and grinned. "I don't look as good as you two do. But that's probably because you two look as if you were going to a club." His eyes lingered at my legs. "The sight of your legs still kills me."

I punched his arm, hard and teasingly. "Oh, come on! You know how I am in long dresses. I swear to God, it's as if my feet disappear under that mess!" I nagged. Boota started to giggle, trying not to make a lot of sound.

But Siddiqis on the other hand let out a good, hearty laugh. Siddiqis's laugh was a laugh of pure joy, yet it also had a menacing theme to it. That's what I loved about him. After, he grinned at me. "This may be my welcome party and all, but it's so boring with a capital B! I know this great club that's not far from here, so you two want to crash it?" he asked, his eyes twinkled devilishly.

I turned to Boota and she shrugged.

Then I turned back to Siddiqis, who was waiting for an answer. "We would love to! Let's leave in ten minutes. I need to take care of something." I took Boota by the hand and placed her hand in Siddiqis's hand. "Can you stay with Boota?" I asked him.

He looked me in the eye. "I'd do anything for you, Rumblen. Anything." He took my hand with his spare and kissed each of my fingers.

I felt a familiar rush coarse through my vein and I kept a straight face. I thanked him and walked deeper into the hall. It had been so long since I've heard anyone call me by my birth name. Only people close to me were allowed to call me Rumblen. A memory suddenly surged into my mind: Siddiqis and I in a dark room, my room. I was lying on the bed, him on top of me. We were kissing, his elbows on both side of my head so he wouldn't crush me, his body on mine, my hands on his shirtless back . . . I quickly dismissed that memory, feeling disgusted with myself. People were dying and I was too busy getting steamy with Siddiqis. That was the night I broke up with him. That was the night before the war. The night before I lost everyone I loved the most. I turned back to see Boota and Siddiqis talking to each other, so I turned away and walked through the crowd, on the search for Angela. I was about to give up looking for Angela until I spotted her next to the wine table, talking to a bunch of vamp guys. I shook my head. When Angela was drunk, she did some crazy things. I was about to walk up to her, until a strong hand clamp around my wrist.

CHAPTER 17

Love Is in the Air

I WHIRLED AROUND to find myself staring into a pair of icy blue eyes. I went still as a statue, trying to keep my breathing calm. Gustav stared down at me, his expression unreadable. "Hello, Kyra," he said in a mature manner. He was wearing a black tuxedo, which gave him a dangerous look. His bangs were pulled back; his eyes were as cold as ice.

"Hello, Gustav," I replied with a surprisingly even tone, "Fancy meeting you here." I fought the urge to pull down my dress, though that would do nothing about his wandering eyes. His stare made me feel naked.

"May I speak to you?" he asked, in a tone that seemed to say I had no choice.

I nodded and still holding my wrist, he led me to a secret door that had a security panel. I watched as he punched in numbers into the panel, and finally, he pushed open the door. The door opened into a hallway I had never seen before. At the end of the hallway was another door. We walked down the hallway and he opened the door. He released my wrist. As we stepped into the room, I took in my surroundings. It was a small room, more like a servant's room. There was a bed, a table, and a TV. I saw that the walls were dark red and that the floor was hard wood. I stepped deeper into the room and heard the room's door close shut and the clicks of locks being turned on. I turned around and almost yelped like a scared puppy. Gustav was standing a few inches away from me, his icy blue eyes staring into my soul. I swore under my breath and stared right back at him. Silence pierced the room, making the room feel smaller than it was.

It was Gustav who broke the silence. "What happened yesterday happened so fast. It was like a blur to me. I've seen Aries get mad, Darq get mad. I get mad for the dumbest things as well. But I've never seen Bonzai get mad. Sure, he gets mad when we fight, but never once has he gotten mad at a woman. He has respect for women, but he doesn't like it when a woman backstabs him," he said in a harsh tone. "Bonzai, Darq, and I aren't so close. But we're brothers. When one gets hurt, the other two knows. Darq and I can take the pain of love or anything, but Bonzai's fragile. He's my younger brother, and even though he doesn't respect me, I love him. Understand?" He had a guarded expression on his face, the same expression he had when he tried to kill me in the Mortal Portal.

I stared back at him with a cold expression. "Did you just call me here so you can make me feel threatened, or do you want to talk like a civilized man?"

He grabbed my bare shoulders harshly. He pulled me closer to him, until we were an inch apart. He smelled like mint and ashes. "I wanted to ask you a question. Who are you going to choose?" he said each word hard, making sure I understood his question.

I tried to hide my temper and looked him in the eye. "Let go of me." I commanded, my tone dripping with venom.

His blue eyes darkened, but he released his hold on my shoulders. Then, like lightning, he knocked me down on the floor, on my back. He was on top of me; his leg captured mine, his face just an inch away from mine. "You allowed Darq and Bonzai to give you a good impression. Now, it's my turn."

Before I could do anything, he had me in a passionate kiss that seemed to last forever. His body was crushing me, but I didn't do anything. He wanted to impress me. I decided to give it a chance. His hands were on my hips, my hands in his hair. He wasn't sloppy like Darq, or soft like Bonzai. He was fierce. I felt a hot rush course through me, as adrenaline surged throughout my veins. I felt the same spark I had felt before with him. After a good five minutes, we pulled away, gasping. I stared up at him, as he stared down at me, his eyes were lit up beautifully.

It was only then a knock on the door broke us out of our trance. Gustav took his time getting off me and went to answer the door as I jumped up and smoothed out my dress. When Gustav opened the door, he gasped in surprise. "How did you get in here?"

The figure pushed him out of the way, which completely surprised me and strolled in. I felt my heart skip a beat. It was Siddiqis. He saw me and walked over to me. "You coming or what?"

I remembered the club and was about to nod, but I realized someone was missing. Then, it hit me. I looked at Siddiqis, panicked. "Where's Boota? You were supposed to be with her!"

He looked at my expression and grinned. "Chill out, Rumblen. She's with Darq. She's dancing with him. You ready or not?"

I stood there, shocked. Darq was dancing with Boota? Then, I grinned to myself. *I guess Darq's finally seeing Boota for who she really is,* I wondered proudly. Then I realized that Siddiqis was waiting with an impatient look on his pretty face. I smiled at him. "I'm ready. But I'm bringing Boota. She needs to experience a club."

Siddiqis grinned. "All right. But if Boota goes, then I think Darq might want to tag along."

"That's good," I said, a playful smile on my lips.

"Where are you guys going?"

We both looked at Gustav, who was looking at us with a confused, frustrated look. Siddiqis gave him a cold look. "We are going to a club. It's called the Bat Cave."

I looked at him and grinned. "The Bat Cave? Didn't you take me there once?"

He chuckled darkly and rubbed his hairless chin. "Yeah. We had some good times there, didn't we?" He turned back to me. His eyes twinkled and I blushed.

Gustav cleared his throat, clearly uncomfortable. "Well, if you, Kyra, Boota, *and* Darq are going to this club, then I'm coming too," he said harshly, "Besides. It's been a long time since I've had some fun." He looked at me, as if waiting for my protest.

But what I said surprised him. "Of course you should come! You need to soften up a bit for the lucky girls there." I grinned at his shocked expression.

"I'm coming too," a voice declared.

We all turned to see Bonzai standing in the doorway, his hands on his hips, staring at me with blazing green eyes.

CHAPTER 18

Surprise, Surprise

I STARED AT him, surprised and horrified. The memory of the scene in the training room popped into my head and I quickly looked away from his gaze.

Siddiqis sighed dramatically. "I guess we're all going then." He looked at me. "Go find Boota and Darq and meet us in the front."

I nodded and slipped past Bonzai, who was still staring at me as I left the hallway. I ran out of the hallway and into the party. I made my way through the crowd of people. When it was clear that they weren't there, I ran out the hall's front doors. I decided to check Darq's room first, and as I walked there, I realized I left my clutch on the floor in the secret room. I smacked my forehead and swore. When I got to Darq's room, the door was closed, but unlocked. I pushed it opened and walked in and then froze.

The scene in front of me knocked all of the air out of me. Darq was on top of Boota, who was on the bed. And they were getting steamy. His shirt was off and Boota's dress was dangerously high with Darq's hand trailing up her thigh. They didn't notice me until I slammed the door shut, knocking them back to reality. Darq jumped off her and stared at me, eyes wide. Boota jumped off the bed, and when she saw it was I, she looked horrified.

"K-Kyra! Oh my god, I – "

"It's all right," I interrupted. "I just didn't expect to walk in while you guys were getting steamy." I grinned, trying not to laugh as I gestured at the crumpled bed.

Boota blushed.

Darq was pale and he looked at me. "Are you really all right with this? Please don't tell Aries about this! He'll fire Boota and her family and I can't stand being without her." He gave Boota a look of protection and love.

"It's all right. I won't tell him, plus I'm actually happy," I said. "Put on a shirt, so we could all go to a club."

"Which one?" he asked.

"The Bat Cave."

He nodded and then threw on a shirt. Boota straightened out her dress and walked over to me. She smiled. "He likes me. Like, he loves me. It's unbelievable."

I grinned at her. "I'm happy for you. Now, what do you say to going clubbing?"

She smiled shyly. "Sure."

Finally, we got to the front doors of the castle, where Siddiqis, Gustav, and Bonzai were waiting. I realized that now I had two only options: marry Gustav or marry Bonzai, since Darq was out of the picture. I sighed. *This is going to be tough*, I thought sadly. As we walked down the stairs, at the three last steps, I tripped because of my stupid high heels. As I went down, I saw a blur, and before I knew it, I was in the arms of Siddiqis, swept off the ground. He grinned down at me. "High heels? Are you serious? Haven't you learned anything from what happened the last time we went dancing and you wore those wedges that were six inches high? Let me take those for you and let's just go barefoot, shall we?" He settled me down on the steps and removed my shoes and helped me up. I thanked him and then saw the look on Bonzai's and Gustav's faces. Gustav looked uncomfortable, and Bonzai glared at us, eyes blazing with something I haven't seen before. *Jealousy*, I realized, as I stepped into the black Honda.

CHAPTER 19

Jealous Boys Finish Last

WE WERE ALL inside Siddiqis's black Honda, and since Siddiqis was driving, I knew we'd be at the club in seconds. And we were. Next thing I knew was that we were at the front of the club. We all got out of the car, and as Siddiqis handed his car keys to a car parker, I saw that the club didn't change a bit. In big letters on top of the club, "The Bat Club" shone brightly. I took in the smell of alcohol and sweat. The music from the club was blaring so loud, I saw Boota covering her ears. I would have too, if I weren't so used to it. I went clubbing many times, but the Bat Cave was possibly my favorite club to go to. They had great non-alcohol drinks and great music. Plus, anybody could get in.

I felt a strong hand on my shoulder. I turned my head to see it was Siddiqis grinning at me. "Remembering the good times, are we?"

I smiled. "Yeah. I love this place. It's always been the best club to go to."

He nodded and motioned for the others, who were talking to each other, to follow us inside. There was no bouncer, so we all just waltzed in and the dance music welcomed us. I turned to see Darq take Boota by the hand, and he looked at me as if to ask permission to go dance.

I nodded and then, they were gonc inside the crowd. I turned to Gustav. "Want a drink?"

He gave me an uncertain look, and then Bonzai turned to me. "I want a drink," he said, his green eyes flashed, as if to challenge me to say no to escorting him.

I stared at him and then motioned for him to follow me, not wanting him to think I was uncomfortable around him even though I was. As we walked through the crowd toward the bar, I felt Bonzai's warm breath on the back of my neck. I led him to the bar and was about to greet the bartender when I saw who the bartender was and my jaw dropped. "Aleks? Aleks Silvermoon?"

The bartender stared at me, registering who I was, and then smiled widely. "Kyra! It's been so long since you've came here! How's the life of a princess?" His thick New York accent told me he visited Earth and stayed in New York City for a while. Aleks hadn't change a bit. He was still skinny, 118 years old, too young to work in a club, though he had grown taller. He had strange yellow cat eyes, and once in a while his fingers let out blue static, which marked him as a warlock. We met in high school, and we always met at the bar with his girlfriend and Siddiqis. Though the two broke up.

I grinned at my old friend. "Still hard, but I'm going a little under the radar. Give me a Vamp Wing, mixed with water of course. My friend here won't drink alcohol." I looked at Bonzai. "Right?"

He was staring at Aleks, completely ignoring me. He kept glaring at him and spoke in a voice dripping with venom. "Are you one of Kyra's ex-boyfriend, or are you one of those poor suckers she made love with and declared you're only friends?"

Aleks was as shocked as the expression on his face, then he spoke in a hard tone. "Listen, buddy. Kyra and I are close friends. Nothing more. So don't you go potty mouthing at people you just met, thinking that they made love with someone, all right? Now take your goddam drink and get out of my face." Aleks slid the drink toward Bonzai as blue static came out of his fingers.

I looked at Aleks, eyes wide and apologetic. "I am so sorry, Aleks. I'll take him away from you. It was nice seeing you again."

"You too, Kyra. Stay safe." He turned away to address the other drinkers.

I took Bonzai's drink and threw it into Bonzai's hands. I glared at him. "What's wrong with you? How dare you accuse Aleks like that? He's my friend and that's all. If you came here to insult me, then good luck. I'm here to party, so suck it up! I thought I should've apologize for what happened yesterday, but now I know that there's no point." I turned and walked away from him, leaving Bonzai to look after me with a guilty look on his face, tears threatened to make an appearance. I fought my way through the crowd of people, searching for a friend. I knew that Darq and Boota were probably making out or dancing, so I searched for old friends, deciding I didn't want to look for Gustav either. Then I felt a hand on my shoulder. I turned to find myself staring into a pair of magenta eyes.

Siddiqis looked at my face and worry crossed his. "What happened, Rumblen? Why are you crying?"

I sniffed. "Just hug me."

He spread out his arms, inviting me back into his arms just like old times. "Come here."

CHAPTER 20

Just like Old Times, but Newer

I SAGGED AGAINST Siddiqis, letting him wrap me in his strong arms like a protective wall around me. I buried my face into his suit, taking in the smell of damp dirt mixed with mint. He whispered soothing words in a different language I couldn't recall. We just stood in that position until he took my wrist and led me to our old secret room, located in the shadows where no one bothered to explore. We slipped through the door into the room. It was pitch black until Siddiqis turned on the switch, and the room's dim light went on. The room was exactly the same as it was the last time we were there together. It had turquoise walls and hard wood flooring, as well with the furniture. There was a queen-size bed in the right corner of the room, and I allowed Siddiqis to lead me to the bed. We sat down on it, him on my right, and after a second, he wrapped his left arm around my shoulders and pulled me closer to him until we touched. I placed my head into his neck hollow, where it fitted like a puzzle piece.

He patted my head, soothingly. "What happened, Rumblen?"

I sniffed. "Bonzai, he – "

"What did he do?" His eyes darkened with protection. "Did he hurt you? What did that spoiled prince do to you?"

I shook my head. "No. He didn't hurt me like that. He thought that Aleks was one of my ex-boyfriends."

"Oh. Now that's harsh," he said, with an angry tone. "Does he know about what happened between us?"

I thought for a second. "I don't know. I think he's jealous, for some bizarre reason, and he thinks that he has to make a big choice. *I'm* the one who has to marry someone to keep peace between the kingdoms! All he has to do is carry on with his day. But all he is doing is trying too hard. He tries acting like someone he's not. He just doesn't get it." I paused. Just then memories came to me: Bonzai saving me from Gustav, Bonzai crying over the fact his mother was gone, Bonzai holding one of my daggers to my neck, Bonzai kissing me on the training room floor, and Bonzai, a hurt look on his face right before he said he never wanted to talk to me again. I shook my head. "Oh god. What have I gotten myself into?"

Siddiqis turned me around until I was staring into his eyes, a light magenta with a hint of hazel. "You can worry about that another time. But tonight's our night." He saw me freeze. "Rumblen, please. Just one more time."

It was risky. I knew Siddiqis used to be my boyfriend, but that seemed ages ago. But I needed a break. No, I needed to be *distracted*. I nodded and I lay down on my back, on the bed.

Siddiqis grinned and took off his suit's blazer. Slowly, he climbed on top of me, his legs trapping mine, his body crushing my body but I didn't care. He leveled his face with mine, our noses touching. He hovered there for a second and then lowered his mouth on to mine. His kisses were experienced, always savoring each one. I felt his love coarse through my veins. He went soft for only a minute, but soon he grew tired of holding back and went hard and fierce. His hands were on my thighs, mine in his hair. After three minutes his hand inched higher.

We stopped kissing and stared at each other. He looked down at me. "Can we?" he asked, his eyes pleading.

I widened my eyes. I never thought about doing it. I knew he always wanted to take it to the next level but I always stopped him. But all I was thinking about was Siddiqis. "Yes, but carefully."

He was breathing hard and nodded. We started kissing again, this time our mouths pressed harshly together. A surge of longing rushed over me. My hands raced to unbutton his white shirt, but my strength caught a hold of me and I ripped his shirt off, tossing it aside. Siddiqis stroked his hand up and down my thigh roughly, yet passionately. Both of us were stronger than any creature because we were hybrids of the most powerful demons and creatures. We both knew what we were doing was dangerous, but we still went hard. My hands explored his shirtless back, as he started kissing my neck, intensively. I moaned in pleasure, and when he started kissing me on the lips again, I felt the prick of his fangs. He must have been excited and I must have been too because I felt my fangs shoot out. We knew how to kiss around fangs, so we kept going. I knew that by the time we were done making out, we would both be bruised, head to toe. I felt as if I couldn't breathe; we were getting steamy. All I thought about was Siddiqis and how good it was to feel him again, one last time. But I also felt how wrong the kiss felt. We would have kept going, if someone hadn't broken open the room's door.

CHAPTER 21

Trouble

SIDDIQIS JUMPED OFF me and bared his fangs at the figure that was standing in the doorway. The figure stepped into the room and slammed the remaining parts of the door shut behind him. As I sat, I saw who it was. I wish I hadn't. Bonzai stared at me, then Siddiqis. His eyes were a raging emerald, and if looks could kill, I was sure to be deader than I am. He glared at us. "What were you two doing? Why aren't you looking?"

Siddiqis looked at him with a cold mature look, mixed with confusion. "Looking for what, your dignity? Cause that was long gone the second you broke the door." He gestured grandly toward the door, which had splintered at the hinges, yet it looked like it still was in working condition.

Bonzai's jaw tightened. "No. For Boota and Darq."

Siddiqis chuckled darkly, which would have sent a shiver up my neck if I were Bonzai. "Why are you looking for the lovebirds? I suggest you quit it because they may be busy." He rubbed his chin, a habit he had even though his face was smooth like a baby's butt. "Very busy."

Bonzai looked like he wanted to kill Siddiqis, but was holding back. "You never answered my first question."

"I told you. We can't find your dignity," he replied with a devilish grin and I resisted the urge to giggle.

"Not that, the first question! What were you two doing?" Bonzai's patience seemed to turn into rage.

"None of your business."

"What do you mean 'none of my business'?"

"Nothing you should be concerned about."

"I'm concerned about Kyra. Plus, as I passed this part of the club, I heard her moaning. So I thought someone was hurting her. What were you doing?"

"Well, I'm concerned about Rumblen too, and she's in perfectly good hands in the moment, so why don't you find yourself a good vamp to dance with?"

Bonzai's face was replaced from a look of anger to a look of confusion and a look of jealously. "Why do you call Kyra 'Rumblen'?"

Siddiqis looked at him, as if he were the dumbest person he had ever met. "That's her birth name. Kyra *Rumblen* Count. Besides, only people very close with her calls her 'Rumblen' because there's a matter of trust that comes with the name." He turned to grin at me and then turned back to Bonzai with a superior look on his pretty cocky face.

Bonzai eyes flashed mad ivy green. "I thought you were her ex-boyfriend. That means she broke up with you because there was a lack of trust she had in you. So tell me. How does it feel to know that the girl you love the most may be in love with another man?" His voice was dripping with venom, and his tone was challenging.

Siddiqis stood there, still as a statue. Then it happened in a flash. Siddiqis lunged at Bonzai, knocking him over. As soon as they hit the ground, I realized that it would have been okay if Siddiqis *wasn't* a powerful demon hybrid and that he couldn't have broken Bonzai's pretty face with just one blow. Unfortunately, Siddiqis *was* a powerful demon hybrid with incredible strength, intelligence, and speed, and he could've broken Bonzai's pretty face with one blow.

I leaped off the bed and yanked Siddiqis off Bonzai. If I were a normal hybrid, then I wouldn't have been able to pull him off. But because I was the same ranking of him, I was able to at least toss him on the floor away from Bonzai and I jumped on top of him. I landed on his chest, pinning his hand over his head, and gasped. The cocky, funny Siddiqis was gone and replaced with a mad, sinister Siddiqis. No one except for me could tell if he was gone. It was because we were linked together by the demons. So when I saw that his eyes were pitch black, including the white part of his eyes, I knew that the demon was in control. *Oh boy, this isn't going to be good,* I thought. The last time the demon was in control of Siddiqis was when a vamp started flirting with me and Siddiqis killed the vamp. I was flattered and horrified that night.

Siddiqis, or should I say the demon, snarled and let out a menacing roar. His body started shaking and I knew Siddiqis's soul was trying to fight the demon in his mind.

I looked over my shoulder and saw Bonzai standing, looking terrified. "Go! Leave before you get him even angrier!" I shrieked at him, struggling to keep the demon on the floor.

In that second, Bonzai ran out the door, leaving me with my old demon boyfriend.

I turned my attention back to the demon, realizing that he was turning gray. I shook my head, panicked and pleading. "No, Siddiqis. Fight the demon harder. You did it before, so you can do it again. Don't let it take over. Please don't give up. Please, please, please. Think about me. Think about our memories. Please don't leave me – "

The demon let out another roar that sounded painful. Then Siddiqis's body stopped shaking and he closed his eyes. He went limp under me. The demon was gone. I didn't just know; I felt it disappear back into the Void, where all demons were. I held my breath as he opened his eyes, as if he had just woken up. His eyes were back to their cocky magenta color, and I exhaled with relief.

Siddiqis stared up at me and then smiled. "You saved me."

I released his hands and cupped his face in my hands. "You're all right. I was so scared I lost you this time," I said, shaking with relief.

He grinned at me. "I would never leave you, Rumblen. Never."

I let out a shaky breath and got off him. I helped him up and then we heard someone open the door. We turned to see Darq carrying Boota, their backs facing us, and they were giggling to themselves. Darq nudged the door shut with his foot, and when he turned and saw us, he swore and dropped Boota, his hands up. Boota landed on the floor on her butt and yelped in pain. She looked up at Darq and scowled, but when she saw us, she got to her feet and blushed.

Darq looked at a shirtless Siddiqis and I, and smiled shyly. "Sorry, I thought the guy at the bar said that this room wasn't taken."

Siddiqis and I exchanged looks, and then Siddiqis looked at Darq and grinned. "Damn. Finding a room, are you? I'm not even going to ask you why." He threw on his torn shirt and just like that, what happened a few seconds ago became the past that was to never be brought back up.

CHAPTER 22

Back to Work

AFTER DANCING FOR a while, we all decided to ditch the party before someone saw that we were missing. We hopped into Siddiqis's Honda and arrived at the castle within seconds. As we walked inside, I saw that everything seemed to be all right. Siddiqis's welcome party was over and the servants were cleaning up the mess. Darq, Bonzai, and Gustav all headed to their rooms, and Boota went straight to her room, not without a goodnight kiss from Darq of course. Siddiqis walked me to my room, and surprisingly, he pulled out my clutch. He handed me it and I took my keys and opened the door. When I was going to close the door, Siddiqis wasn't ready to leave.

He braced both of his hands on either side of the doorway, making me unable to close the door. He grinned. "Had a good time?"

I smiled. "I always have a good time when I go clubbing with you."

He chuckled darkly. "I'm staying in the room across the hall. If you need me, think about my eyes." He tried making a seductive face, but failed miserably and settled for a smirk.

"You're so pathetic." I laughed, putting a hand on his chest and lightly pushed him, only he didn't move.

He shot me a wink. "Good night, Rumblen." He, then, leaned toward me and kissed the top of my head. Then, he was gone.

I shut the door and collapsed onto my bed. I was asleep in an instant, dreaming about a time I had no responsibilities.

* * *

The next day hit me hard. I realized that I would have to eat at a table with the Deatheye family again and groaned. I got ready and decided to wear a bright yellow dress. I accessorized and then declared I wasn't going to wear shoes, figuring that no one really cared about it. I smacked on lip-gloss, grabbed my keys and clutch, and I was out the door. I walked down to the dining hall and threw open the doors. I saw Aries and Siddiqis laughing, as Gustav and Bonzai remained silent. Darq was staring at Boota, who was in her maid's outfit holding a pitcher of water. Boota was avoiding Darq's gaze, as if shy. As I took a seat between Siddiqis and Darq, I noticed that the boys were all wearing training gear, similar to my own that was locked in my luggage.

Siddiqis turned to me and smiled, his eyes wide and bright. "Good morning. What a dress!"

Aries smiled brightly. "Kyra, I hope you slept well."

I looked at Aries and grinned. "Like the dead, actually."

He shot me a silly look mixed with a playful scowl and then clapped his hands twice. A crowd of servant came into the room with plates of food.

After eating my full, I pushed back my plate and dabbed my mouth with a napkin. "Aries?"

Aries looked at me over his wine glass. "Yes, Kyra?"

"I think I'm going to the Xercus library. I need to do some research about this battle." I really needed to get started on trying to stop this upcoming battle before it gets out of hand.

Siddiqis looked at me, stunned. "What do you mean?"

I looked at him, confused. "I thought Angela told you. Someone is trying to create another battle, this time our kingdoms against an army of demons."

"No. She told me. I just didn't know that she wasn't kidding about the army of demons part. I came here right away to find out if it's true. Now, I know why Aries called me here." He rubbed his chin in thought.

Gustav and Bonzai looked up from their plates at the same time, shocked, and stared at me. Gustav was the first to speak. "Another battle? How is that possible? Only powerful hybrids can summon an army of demons! And the only powerful hybrids are you and Siddiqis."

Siddiqis rubbed his temple. "That's not true. There are other powerful hybrids, but we are all different because we are all from different types of creatures. Rumblen is the hybrid of a powerful vampire and mother of all demons, Lilith. God bless their souls. But Rumblen does have some ancient angel powers in her. So she isn't pure evil or pure angel. I am the hybrid of an avenging angel, also known as a dark angel, and Satan's younger brother. And since my father helped Heaven at one point, an angel made sure I wouldn't be pure evil. So I'm neither too. But there are some who are pure evil, so they may be who is trying to summon demons."

Gustav's eye widened. "You're part avenging angel?"

Siddiqis gave him a hard look. "Be happy that you had good parents. If you didn't have Luna as a mother, then you may have turned evil. God bless her soul. And Aries is possibly the only reason you can control your powers now."

Gustav looked at him, confused. "I still don't get how you're not pure evil."

Siddiqis looked at him, annoyed. "I'm just not, okay? If I were, why would I be here?" He snapped.

Bonzai glared at him. "Why are you here?"

The scene from last night came rushing at me and I was quick to dismiss it.

Siddiqis looked at Bonzai, as if he just noticed his presence. "Aries called me here to help train you guys. I've learned many things and I'm willing to teach you guys," he said in a superior tone.

Aries stood up and cleared his throat. "I have a meeting with the fey clan, so Siddiqis is in charge. Kyra, you should get a head start if you want to get to the library unspotted. I'll see you at dinner." He nodded at me and then walked out of the room. We were all silent.

I broke the silence by standing up. "If you'll excuse me, I'll be at the library." I didn't even wait for them to answer; instead, I ran out of the room.

CHAPTER 23

Undercover

I RAN BACK to my room to grab my black leather jacket, threw on some sunglasses and slipped on my black Converse. I decided not to bring my clutch, so I grabbed a black messenger bag and threw my room key into it, knowing that it would be easier to haul books in the bag. I locked my room door and dashed to the front door of the castle. I pulled it open and ran out. The fresh spring air hit me and I took in the smell of roses. Even though Xercus was a dead kingdom, there were some spots that had life. I walked down the sidewalk, and when a servant came insisting to drive me to the library, I refused.

As I continued to walk down the gray sidewalk, I saw houses. The houses were small, with only one floor and possibly a basement if some were lucky. I saw that there was only one supermarket and that there were more than three clubs. But the thing that bothered me the most was people. Most were vamps, hobgoblins, and warlocks, and I noticed that the fey clan must have been secretive and that the werewolf clan was far away from the vamp headquarters was a run-down police station. Surprisingly, most of the people weren't half bad looking. But I knew that by the way they walked and slammed their doors, that they weren't as happy as my citizens back in my kingdom. I walked with my hands in my jacket's pockets, head down. I didn't want anybody to recognize me as the princess who almost slayed their entire kingdom, including their loved ones. After a few minutes of walking, I finally arrived at the library. I looked up, amazed.

The library was a tall big gray building that was made up of ancient stone. At the very top of the library were two gargoyles, one on either side, peering down with sickening expressions. I shuddered at them, feeling their stone eyes stare into my soul. I marched up the library's steps and pulled open the front doors. The second I stepped in, I smelt the rusting of ancient books. Books lined up against the wall, all rustic looking, all with a piece of history in them.

I was broken out of thought when I heard someone was tapping with a foot impatiently. I looked to my left to see an old lady behind a big wooden desk and realized that she was the librarian. She had white hair and wrinkled shin. Her eyes were ivy green, and she seemed to be nice unlike many mean old ladies. I smiled at her, sweetly. "Good morning, ma'am."

The lady stared at me with questioning eyes. "Who are you? Clearly I haven't seen you here before." She spoke with in a raspy, unkind manner. I knew right there I wasn't as good as my mother at judging people by their looks.

I kept my sunglasses on and tried to appear relaxed. "I just came to town, looking for a new start. Is there any chance you can help me find a book?"

The lady didn't appear to have bought my explanation. "What are you?"

I tried looking as innocent as possible. "I'm full vamp. May I ask what you are?"

The lady nodded, a look of approval on his aging face. "I'm a witch. Of course, I've never seen a young vamp travelling by herself. Are you a rogue?" Her eyes were inspecting every bit of me.

I shook my head. "Oh no! I'm not a rogue. I just felt like visiting the kingdom."

"Take off your sunglasses," she commanded.

I blinked. "I beg your pardon?"

"Take off your glasses," she repeated, this time I heard a hint of annoyance.

I kept my face expressionless. "Ma'am, I'm still sensitive to light – "

"Take off your glasses!" she yelled.

I jumped back a little, surprised that such an old lady had such a strong voice. This woman looked older than sixty-five. Of course she couldn't have been older than me because I was 118, and she was just a witch and they died like humans. Unless she was an offspring of a warlock, which was impossible. I cleared my throat. "Ma'am, please. I dread the light."

Her eyes darkened. "I shall not allow you to leave or read until you remove your sunglasses. By all means, you could be a rogue. Remove them this instant!" Her voice echoed through the library, proving that no one was present except for us. She was suspicious about me, and if I were this lady, I'd be too. Full vamps are rarely sensitive to sunlight, but we were inside, so I guessed this witch knew that I wouldn't be affected. But I knew that if I removed my sunglasses, this woman would see my eyes. Since I'm a powerful hybrid, my eyes have a weird glow to them. I have light gray eyes that are mysterious, not really a weird thing. But this weird glow marks me as demon hybrid and a powerful one at that.

I hesitated for a second and then sighed, giving up. “Fine, but don’t freak out,” I warned the lady. I pulled off my sunglasses and felt my eyes flash.

The lady gasped, a bony hand sprawled across her chest. “Kyra? Kyra Rumblen Count?”

I smiled. “That’s me.”

Then she did something that shocked me. She started to laugh menacingly. Then she grinned at me. “Honey, we thought that you were smarter. You’re making this too easy.”

I looked at her, confused and alarmed. “*We?*” I looked around and started to back up. That’s when I bumped into someone. Instantly, a dagger was at my neck, held by the person behind me. I swore under my breath. It was a trap.

The person behind me chuckled darkly and spoke in a low voice that dripped with venom, telling me he was male. “Kyra Rumblen Count. My boss told me you’re a special girl, and that it would be hard to kill you. But he never said anything about you being hard to hurt.”

I felt a dagger he held go away from my neck and felt it plunge into my back, and through my spine. I looked down to see the tip of the dagger sticking out of my stomach. I gasped, from shock and pain, and felt my world tilted. Then, everything went dark.

CHAPTER 24

Captive

I WOKE UP, feeling as if I had just crawled out of my grave again. Suddenly, the events that occurred before I passed out played through my mind. I sat up quickly and instantly regretted it. I felt as if I was dying all over again and maybe I was. I fully opened my eyes and saw that I was in a prison cell except that it wasn't in a prison. It was in the library's basement. I looked around, taking in the room's surroundings. The cell was actually huge, cold and damp, and its emptiness made me feel small. It was all stonewalls and stone floor and there was nothing in the room except for me. No windows, no way out. I tried to push strands of hair out of face but soon realized that my hands were tied behind my back with some kind of metal I couldn't break out of. My legs weren't tied together, so I was able to walk. Actually, I wasn't considering walking due to the fact that my legs felt like jelly. I suddenly felt pain in my stomach and looked down to see I was still bleeding from the stab. I looked around, panicked. I was in a basement with a lunatic old witch and a guy wielding a dagger. After trying to break free of the metal around my wrist, which was all scratched up, I gave up and decided to make a plan. *Pull it together, Kyra. The boys at the castle knew where you were going. Once they realize that you've been missing for a while, they'll come to your aid,* I told myself. Then I realized that if they came and asked the old lady where was I, she could lie or capture them too. I groaned and then stopped. *Siddiqis,* I thought, *we're connected hybrids. That means I should be able to contact him with my mind and create a hologram to talk to him.* I sat up, ignoring the piercing pain, and crossed my legs. I remembered all of my training about the spirit world and told myself that all of that training prepared me for this. I relaxed my mind and thought of Siddiqis. I focused on sending my soul out of my body and going to Siddiqis. After a minute, I was successful. I hovered over my body, which was posed as if I was meditating. I looked down to see that I looked exactly like my body and squealed with victory. I then flew up, out of the building, and when I got outside, I flew straight to the castle. When I got there, I just went right through the door. There were servants in the foyer, but none saw me because I was invisible. At a time like that, I would have been pulling down people's pants, but I had to get to Siddiqis. I floated around the castle until I was at Siddiqis's door. I went through the door.

Siddiqis's room was as big as my own. He had the same décor except his vanity dresser and mirror table had gear on it. His bed was messed up, the blankets showed that he had a rough night, and his clothes were tossed onto the floor. I heard a door open and Siddiqis came out of his bathroom, a towel covering his personal part. He was shirtless and his hair was wet. The room was instantly filled with an aroma of citrus soap and it felt hot. Siddiqis walked over to the bed and I was confused. *Why can't he see me?* I wondered, confused and frustrated. I waved a hand in front of his face, but he didn't know I was there. I cursed. I was invisible to him too. *Great job, genius! You're a ghost!* I thought with an irritated growl. Siddiqis picked up his cell phone and dialed a number. He held up the phone to his ear and waited.

A quiet hello came from the phone and Siddiqis's face grew serious. "Did the plan work?"

There was a pause as he listened.

Then he grinned. "Perfect. Are you sure she can't come out until I get there?"

Another pause.

"Okay, don't screw up. We need her to be locked up until it's over."

What's over? What is he talking about and whom is he talking to? I wondered.

Siddiqis nodded. "Good. She has no idea what's going on! Can you believe it? For such a pretty girl, she's awfully dumb." He laughed darkly.

He listened to the person on the other side.

Then he went dead serious. "Must I repeat the plan to you, you stubborn witch? You're going to put your henchman in charge of her and you're going to cast a spell to set the demons free. I'm going to take care of her, say she's dead, and then we'll attack Xercus while they're weak. After, we'll attack the Mortal Portal kingdom, and soon, the world. Right now, I'm on my way to you and I guess it's time to break it to her."

A pause.

"All right. Bye." He hung up and grinned to himself. Then he had disappeared into the bathroom again, humming to himself.

I floated there, trying to gather my thoughts in my head. *Cast a spell? Set the demons free? Attack Xercus and then the Mortal Portal? What's going on?* I wondered, trying to bring the puzzle pieces together. I felt myself float out of Siddiqis's room, out of the castle, into the cell, and back into my body. I gasped for air as I got back into my body, and instantly, I felt pain from my wound. I tried to clear my mind, but I realized that I didn't tell him I was here, trapped by an old witch hag and her henchman.

I heard my cell door open and I looked up to see a man, big and tall. He was slightly tanned and had silver dead eyes that pierced my soul but I refused to flinch under his stare.

He grinned down at me through his tousled brown hair. "Hello again. I'll be keeping you company until my boss comes here."

I eyed the man and realize that he was the one who had stabbed me. I looked at him coldly. "Who's your boss? And what does he or she want from me?" I winced at the pain from my wound.

The man eyed me and then looked at me as if I were a rare animal. "I guess you're mad I stabbed you, huh?"

"Well, at least you know half the reason why I'm mad at you. Who's your boss?" I struggled against the metal that tied my hands together.

"You can go now, Hugo. I got it covered," a voice had said.

I stopped struggling and looked up to see a figure in the doorway behind the man, Hugo. Hugo nodded and then stalked out of the room. The figure walked into the room and closed the door. He locked it and then turned to me.

That's when I saw his face and my heart dropped. I felt like throwing up and I urged myself to stay calm. But how was I supposed to stay calm when I saw who it was?

He came toward me and bended down until we were eye to eye. He chuckled darkly. "Surprise, Rumblen." His breath reeked of blood and mint. I felt so many emotions but one stood out: betrayal.

I stared into the magenta eyes of my dear friend Siddiqis.

CHAPTER 25

The Truth

I FROZE, STARING in shock. I gulped and cleared my voice. "Siddiqis? What's going on?" I said every word slowly, afraid that if I spoke too fast I would break down crying.

Siddiqis grinned at me and cocked his head to the head. "I would tell you what's going on, but I'm just waiting for *you* to realize what's going on." He waited; his magenta eyes took in my status. I saw he was wearing new training gear: a black leather sleeveless jacket and black leather pants complimented with a belt that held knives, daggers and his sword that he only used for wars and battles. He was also wearing short boots, a dagger hilt showing and its blade disappeared into his boots. In this gear, he looked even more frightening when his magenta eyes flashed.

I looked him in the eye. "You're helping create an uprising."

He groaned as if he were hoping I said something else. "Oh dear, Rumblen. How stupid are you? I'm not *helping* to create an uprising. *I'm* the one who's leading this plan." His eyes twinkled menacingly.

I was dizzy and I felt breakfast making its way up my throat, but I swallowed it down. I struggled to keep my voice steady. "You?" I shook my head. "Why, Siddiqis? Why all of this? You have everything you ever wanted. Why?" I asked him, feeling as if he had just punched me in the stomach. I looked down, refusing to look him in the eye.

He looked at me. "Rumblen, look at me."

I continued to ignore him.

"Rumblen – "

"Don't call me that. You have no rights to call me by my birth name. You said it yourself. Only people that have earned my trust could call me that!" My voice came out hoarse, rising up into a shout.

That got Siddiqis angry. He took my chin and forced me to look up at him. "Look at me!" he demanded.

So I did. His magenta eyes were blazing and I felt my energy slink away. "You will look me in the eye as I tell you what I plan to do. Is that clear?" He spoke in a tone that dripped with venom.

I tried to tear my gaze off his, but his hand was gripping my chin hard, making me look at him against my will. That was the first time I had ever wish I could kick him in the shins. But I couldn't. Instead, I spoke. "I only have one question for you."

"And what's that, my dear?" His voice was mockingly sweet and challenging.

"How do you plan to use a spell to free all of the demons to take over the world? Even you know that takes a powerful witch to do that." I stared at him in the eye.

He appeared confused and startled. Then he chuckled quietly. "You used our connection and gave me a little visit when I was on the phone, didn't you? I hope you didn't see me without a towel on. But maybe you wanted to." He grinned like the devil he was.

I ignored his last comment and rolled my eyes. "Give me an answer, Starburn."

He rubbed his chin with his free hand. "Starburn, huh? Don't feel like using the first names, do you? All right, Rumblen, I'll tell you the plan." He sat down crossing his legs, one of his hands still on my chin, forcing me to look at him since he was slightly taller even when sitting. "After the war, all I was thinking about was *you.* I thought that since the war was over, you'd come running back into my arms. But you chose your kingdom over me. So when I heard you were going to marry one of the Deatheye princes, I was mad and hurt. I wanted revenge, and vengeance would be mine. I started contacting the demons, asking them to assist me in a battle against Xercus and the Mortal Portal and then the world. When Aries asked me to come to train his boys, I only agreed to get close to you and weaken the three princes. But when I saw you at my welcoming party, I fell in love with you all over again. I decided to give you a chance to prove that you belonged to me. So I waited for you to come back. That night we were together and getting steamy, I thought you were going to be mine again. But when that idiot Bonzai burst in, he ruined everything. So I let the demon inside of me try to kill him. Unfortunately, you pulled me off and got the demon out. I then knew that you loved me as if I were a brother to you and that you cared for Bonzai, Gustav, and Darq more. Today, after you left the dining hall, I told the boys to meet me in the training room for training. I left them and retreated back to my room to tell Linda, the old witch, that you were going to her library and that you had to be captured. Linda's been alive for a long time and knows how to summon demons, to answer your previous question. But of course, she needs the blood of a powerful hybrid and I'm more than happy to lend her some of my own. Anyways, back to what happened after you left, I went to the training room and struck a deal with the three fools."

"What kind of a deal?" I asked, fearing the worst.

Siddiqis grinned. "I told them that if one of the three were able to knock down my sword, I'd leave and never talk to you again. Nothing was supposed to happen if they weren't able to unarm me. So after an hour of trying to unarm me at the same time, they still failed. Of course, I didn't care whether they won or not. I just needed to weaken them. As soon as the three princes fell to the floor, exhausted, I tied them, gagged them, and put them inside the room's closet." He laughed darkly. "You should have seen Gustav's face when I closed the door. What a look of rage! I'm pretty sure they're okay, just a little sore and pissed." He saw the look I gave him. "Aw, come on, Rumblen! Don't look at me with those judging big eyes. Be happy I didn't kill them as much as I would like to. I only allowed them to live because of you." He moved to tuck a strand of my hair behind my ear, but I bared my teeth at him like a caged tiger. He let my chin go and stood up. I stared up at him, in horror and shock. The Siddiqis I grew up with turned into a monster. Memories flashed before my eyes: Siddiqis and his father, when he was a child, walking toward my family and I, Siddiqis throwing me into a lake because I drank all of his apple juice, Siddiqis holding me when I fell and scraped my knee when we were young, Siddiqis and I under the willow tree at my kingdom, him telling stories about his glorious fight against rogue werewolves, Siddiqis and I in high school sharing an apple, Siddiqis and I in my room getting steamy, Siddiqis's hurt expression when I broke up with him, Siddiqis at his welcoming party, Siddiqis catching me when I fell from the stairs at Xercus, Siddiqis kissing me passionately, and finally, Siddiqis telling me he would never leave me. Now, I stared up at a monster that looked exactly like the boy I used to care about. *Love is dangerous, child. Never be fooled by one's previous actions, for the secrets inside the person creates them*, my mother had said before the war. I never cared about what my mother had to say about love because I thought that love wasn't ever dangerous when mixed in with Siddiqis. Now, I beg to differ.

Siddiqis stared down at me, his eyes full of cruelty. "I could just leave you here to bleed to death, but that wouldn't be the right way for the princess of the Mortal Portal to die." His eyes were a scary magenta, and he grinned cruelly, sending shivers up my back. "Instead, I'll make you a deal." When I didn't protest, he continued. "I'll let you go, only if you join me against the fools in Xercus. Think about it. It makes sense! We are the most powerful hybrids on this world.

Together, nothing could stop us! We are infinite together!" His eyes gleamed wickedly, and he looked even more sinister than he sounded.

I narrowed my eyes at him. "And if I decline the deal?"

His face darkened. "Then, I'll make you wish you accepted. Your choice, Rumblen." He looked down at me, waiting.

CHAPTER 26

Time to Make a Choice

I INSTANTLY FELT like passing out, but I urged myself to stay conscious. I was at crossroads again: Join my old friend and betray the ones I loved or risk my life for the people that never even liked me? I wanted to get out of there. Suddenly, flashes of memories crossed my mind: Bonzai crying, Gustav kissing me, Darq and Boota exchanging loving glances, Aries and Luna, my parents, my sister, my citizens back at my kingdom, and finally, myself looking into my mirror back in the MP, right before the war that changed my life. I looked up at Siddiqis, who was looking impatiently at me, and smiled sweetly. "Go to hell, Starburn."

Siddiqis's pretty face displayed blazing anger. It was replaced with a pissed look and he sighed sadly. "I was hoping you'd be smarter and that you'd be grateful that I was trying to spare your life. But I see I've just wasted time letting you talk and breathe."

Something slashed the air beside my ear and I saw that he had thrown a knife that stuck into the wall beside me. *Enchanted*, I realized with a gulp, knowing that only enchanted objects could go through anything. I looked back at him.

He was grinning at me. "I missed on purpose. You know I don't like using the knives and daggers as much as I do with strength and my sword." Then he raised my chin up and gripped it so hard, I gasped in pain. He let go and I felt a trail of my blood trickle down my chin and neck. He laughed at my pain and the blood and kicked me in the face. I wanted to clutch my face, but my hands were tied behind my back. I fell to my side on the floor, my cheek against the cold stone, as I tried to fight the pain. He then kicked me in my stomach, right where I was stabbed. I doubled over on the floor, my cheek against the cold stone. I groaned in pain as Siddiqis dragged me out of my precious corner and into the middle of the room. He circled around me, wondering where to strike next. He must have known I was stabbed from the back because he landed a hard kick there. I bit my bottom lip, trying not to scream out and satisfy him with the glorious sounds of weakness. He laughed even more and grinned down at me. "Not hard enough? What about this?" He kicked me multiple times in the stomach, each one harder and harder and harder than before. I felt like I was dying, and the more he kicked me, the more my strength weakened and the wall keeping me from crying threatened to break. Realizing I was so close to breaking, he circled my limp body and kicked me in the stomach again. This time, I couldn't hold in the horrible pain. I screamed and screamed in pain until my throat started to hurt. The pain I felt that day cannot be explained thoroughly with words. It was unlike anything I've had ever felt and it was like dying all over again, this time the agony was uncontrollable and the fear of dying was in place. I closed my eyes and wished that he could have just left me to rot. Siddiqis nudged me with his foot and I rolled over onto my back, moaning. I knew he was grinning even though my eyes were closed, and I felt him kneel down, his face inches from mine, his foul breath pelted my face. I shuddered.

He chuckled. "Oh, Rumblen," he sang in a taunting, menacing voice. I heard him pull out a dagger from his belt and felt it sink into my shoulder, pinning me to the stone ground. I shrieked in pain and agony. He did the same to my other shoulder, and I gritted my teeth so hard, I was pretty sure I chipped a tooth. "Open your eyes and show me that you're not a coward by looking into the eyes of your death."

That's when I felt it. My pain turned into rage, blinding rage toward Siddiqis. I felt the strength of my mother inside of me, and I came up with a plan. I opened my sore eyes and Siddiqis let out a quiet gasp.

I knew why he gasped. It were my eyes, the once calm glowing gray eyes were replaced with two different eye colors. One was a stormy gray and the other was an extraordinary gold, showing the demon and angel within me. Once upon a time, my mother was Adam's wife until she was cursed and turned evil. When I broke her curse of never being able to produce a living baby, an angel gave me some angelic powers. So like a warlock's mark, my eyes were my hybrid mark.

I stared up at my old friend, rage burning in my soul. "You dare call me a *coward*? May I remind you that you're the one who didn't even release me, knowing that there's the chance I could possibly beat you? If you weren't such a coward, you'd release me and fight me like a man. So what are you waiting for, you coward? Kill me while I'm down and defenseless." My voice was hoarse, but still I saw that it held meaning to Siddiqis. I knew reverse psychology had worked on Gustav before and I knew that it would work on Siddiqis too.

He appeared shocked, but collected himself within seconds. His magenta eyes danced wickedly. "All right. Let's lay down some rules, though. No daggers or knives unless the opponent's on the ground. I'll put away my sword and it will be sparing between us. But we are allowed to use our powers." He pulled both daggers out of my shoulders and I felt an instant wave of pain and relief wash over me. He then pulled a key out of his pants pocket and released my hands.

I resisted the urge to wrap my hands around his neck and instead I held a hand to my sore cheek.

"I'll only give you a minute to get yourself up and ready to fight." He got up and backed up as he took off his weapon's belt, discarding it into a corner. As I tried to sit up, I felt my shoulder wounds slowly close up; my vampire blood was helping me recover. Still, as my wounds closed, I was sore and my stomach wound was still killing me, though it was closing up. I sat up and checked to make sure nothing was broken. I wiped the blood away from my chin and got to my feet, painfully. I felt like going down again, but I urged myself to stay strong enough to take on my old friend. I got up and almost collapsed. I stomped both feet on the ground, waking them out of their sleepy condition. I stared at Siddiqis and realized that it came down to that moment. Years of training together had put me in a disadvantage, yet an advantage, because we both knew each other's strengths and weaknesses. Except we didn't know exactly what powers the other person had, which was a bad thing and a good thing. I rubbed my wrists, which were scraped to the point that raw flesh was visible, and then set my hands on my hips, my gaze fully on Siddiqis.

"Ready?" My hands shook and I clenched and unclenched them.

He grinned darkly, sending shivers up my back, and raised his chin. "Ready."

CHAPTER 27

Came Down to this Moment

WE TOOK A few steps backward, our eyes never parting, away from each other. We then circled around the room, keeping a good distance between us. Siddiqis walked with the grace of a panther, slow and taunting, his eyes calculating every step I took. I mirrored his walk, though while he was grinning, I had a determined, serious look on my face. We circled and circled, eyeing each other and trying to figure out who's going to exchange the first attack. Siddiqis's appeared calm, but his eyes showed he was slightly nervous. No. Not that he was nervous. His eyes showed that he was slightly uncomfortable, though his cocky features stood out more, masking that little flaw. I tried to appear relaxed, but I was in a blood-soaked dress that exposed my legs and I was already more tired and restless than him, putting me at a disadvantage. I was shaking with fear and adrenaline. Finally, we stopped circling and ended up where we started. We both were still, and silence pierced the room. At first nothing happened.

Then I felt a horrible pain sear through my head. I ignored it to keep my gaze on Siddiqis, but it got even more painful over time, and in seconds, I was clutching me head in agony. *What's happening*, I wondered as I crippled to my knees, my head still in my hands, and I cried out in blinding pain. I heard Siddiqis laugh menacingly and darkly. *Of course,* I realized, *he's using his powers against me! That's why he was staring at me for a long time, not just to make eye contact with me.* I refused to be overthrown by his tricks. I looked up slowly and looked him in the eye.

He stopped laughing and stared at me, grinning. I gathered whatever energy I had left and attacked his mind, imagining his head exploding. I felt satisfied when I heard him cry out in surprise and pain and land on his knees. Finally, he stopped hurting me, and I stood up and stopped hurting his mind. He stopped holding his head and looked up at me.

Siddiqis growled, a scowl on his pretty face, and stood up. Then, surprising me, he grinned. "Impressive. But face it. You had me down and you could've have killed me. You're too weak, Rumblen. That's why I plan on putting you to sleep." He lunged at me and I tried to move out of the way, but he was too fast. We went flying into the wall behind me and I felt all of my breath in my lungs escape. As I gasped for air, Siddiqis had my back against the cold stone wall, his body pressed against mine, and had his hands around my neck in seconds, cutting off any air from entering my lungs. I clawed at his hands, which was no good, and settled for kneeing him in his nuts. He swore and slapped me hard. My cheek stung and I felt tears threaten to make an appearance, but I refused to cry. I kneed him again, this time much harder and I hoped I bruised him there. Finally, he let go off my neck to hold his injured area with a yelp of pain, looking down to mask his pain, and for a second, I pitied him for having such a weak area. That second didn't last long and I took the opportunity to knee him in the face. A sickening crack broke through the room, which clearly meant I broke his pretty nose. Shouting and swearing, he went down holding his injured nose and I realized I had him down. I instantly dove for one of his abandoned daggers, and when I turned around, he was already up, his wound already healing. His eyes were burning with hatred and rage, and I took a step back, cautiously. He wiped the blood that dripped from his healing nose off his face, quickly, and stared at me, waiting.

I realized we were both panting and I tried to hide how tired I was. "Tired yet?" I touched the back of my head, which had hit the wall hard, and my hand came away bloody. I urged myself to stay conscious and I felt the wound already start to heal itself.

He managed a weak grin. "Oh, please. I've just caught my second wind." Then in the speed of light, he lunged and knocked me down. As I landed on my back, he landed on top of me and wrestled the dagger out of my grip. He then drove the dagger under my heart, missing it by an inch, on purpose. I let out a scream of pure agony, for that was one of my weakest spots. Siddiqis got off me and walked to his abandoned daggers. Realizing what he was doing, I struggled to get the blasted dagger out of me, but it being enchanted, it pinned me to the stone floor. I clawed at the hilt, desperate to get it out. By then, Siddiqis was already towering over me and got on top of me, eliminating the use of my legs. Before I could react, he drove two blades into my shoulders, pinning my arms done, in the same area he stabbed me before. This time, I winced as the blades sank into my shoulders and heard it drive into the floor. I stared up in pain at Siddiqis, who was grinning down at me, his eyes dancing with victory. His forehead was plastered with sweat and blood trickled down his chin. Even bleeding and crazy, he was slightly attractive in a scary way.

He chuckled darkly. "Looks like we're back to square one," he said in an amused tone, "I told you that you stand no match for me, Rumblen. I have to say that you put up a good fight. But let's be honest, darling. You can never beat me. You're too good. Which is why you can't kill me. But I can kill you." He leaned down and leveled his face an inch above mine, his voice dropped low. "It's such a shame you have to die. But don't worry, I'll send a prayer for you to your Angel and Satan. Now, you can be with your family, thanks to me." He sat up and held the dagger with both hands, over his head. "Good-bye, Kyra Rumblen Count."

I didn't close my eyes; it was the right way to die by facing your death in the eyes. I stared him in the eyes, as Siddiqis drove the dagger into my heart, hitting home. I saw my life pass by me as the dagger came down: the day I was born, my mother smiling and cheering with glory as I raised from the dead, Bethela being born, the first time I met Siddiqis, the day I died again to be reborn even more powerful, the day I learned how to fly as a bat, the day I had my first sip of blood from a victim, my first kiss with Siddiqis, Luna and I braiding each other's hair and laughing, Siddiqis and I getting steamy, me breaking his heart, me getting ready for the war that changed my life, my family's funeral, me weeping by Luna's grave, Aries asking me to marry one of his sons, me meeting Gustav for the first time, meeting Bonzai for the first time, meeting Darq for the first time, my first breakfast with the Deatheye family, Darq and I kissing, Angela with her flirtatious grin, Gustav and I kissing in my room, Gustav's face when I told him to go, Bonzai and I kissing in the training room, Bonzai storming out of the room, Boota and I at the party, Siddiqis staring down at me at his party, Gustav and I in the secret room, Darq and Boota kissing, Siddiqis and I kissing at the club and getting steamy, Siddiqis fighting the demon inside him, and the last time I saw the Deatheye boys before I was kidnapped. The last moment I saw was Siddiqis plunging the dagger into my heart, and I realized I had failed not only my country, but Xercus as well. I let out a gasp of surprise and pain as the dagger pierced my heart, and finally, after a few seconds, I felt my heartbeat slowed down, until I stopped breathing. Completely.

CHAPTER 28

Death Is in the Air

I LAY THERE on the cold stone floor, lifeless. My soul drifted out off my body and I peered down at the scene before me. My body was glowing, a sign that my soul had left my body, and I realized that one of my eyes were a different color than the other. Like they were when I was fighting Siddiqis, one golden, the other a stormy gray color. My once yellow dress was soaked with blood, clearly my own, and I felt strange peering down at my body. I had now died three times; the first when I was first born due to my mother's curse of not being able to give birth to a child, yet I broke the curse and became a hybrid; the second time at an shoot-off when I was ten and I came back to life as a full vamp and a stronger hybrid than ever. And now, I died from the hands of my ex-boyfriend. I looked like I was asleep with my eyes opened and I felt a sense of dread wash over me as I shuddered at the fact that I really died. Then I noticed Siddiqis.

He looked shaken up, as if he couldn't believe what had just happened. He also had blood on his gear, mostly mine, and I saw that his magenta eyes were fading to a dead gray, but I knew it was temporary. He was my bad half, so I was his good half that kept him strong and happy. Of course, dying took that away. Now, Siddiqis sat on top of my dead, limp body and he did something that surprised me. He sang in a low mourning voice. "*My sister, my blood. May she lay her head. May the dirt of the past become her bed. May she rest in peace. Her soul will be free. And May the Angel and Satan let her be.*" I felt my dead heart jump. He had sung prayers for me. I thought he would spit on my grave, but instead, he actually sang the sacred prayer of the dead who were bonded to a soul. Siddiqis, then, drew a hand to my face and closed my eyes. He started wiping the blood off of my face, and then, he kissed my forehead. I shuddered at the thought of the touch of his lips on my forehead, the same lips that lied to my face. After a second of looking at my face, he reached for the dagger that was still embedded in my heart and pulled it out. I felt a sharp pain, only for a second, and then I felt nothing. Just emptiness. Then he pulled out all of the daggers, unpinning my limp body from the ground.

Siddiqis then got off my limp, dead body and peered down at it. He was expressionless. "Dear, sweet Kyra Rumblen Count." He knelt down beside my body, his tone low and amused. "I can't believe you had to die this way. I know you probably can't hear me, but I want you to know that it was an honor to know you. We've had many great times, but sometimes, things have to be done. Choices must be made, and you've made bad choice. I might as well tell you what I plan to do next, since you can't do anything at this point." He tucked a strand of my hair behind my ear, smiling at the fact he had won. "I plan on taking you back to the castle, back to the Deatheye family, so you could be buried properly. I'm pretty sure the princes are found by now, so I'll have to try to convince their foolish father that I did it in fear they would kill themselves trying to save you. That sounds heroic, don't you think? I don't expect you to answer, but it's the thought that counts."

Get away from my body, you monster! Dare to touch my body again and I will spit on your grave! I tried to shout, soon realizing he couldn't hear my words. Besides, I was probably going to spit on his grave anyways.

He grinned evilly. "Then, when they see your body, they'll be full of grief and I'll sneak off to free the demons from their prison, the Demon Void. After, I'll attack Xercus and then the Mortal Portal and soon the entire world. Maybe even Earth, if I'm feeling lucky. But I'm sorry to say that when I give your body to the Deatheye family, I'll take off to summon the demons. It's such a shame you don't have anybody to carry on your family legacy. Anyways, I'll try to make the ride to the castle for you as smooth as possible." He picked me up off the ground and my body was limp in his arms.

I wanted to kill him for touching me again, but I knew I couldn't do that. I was a soul out of a body, meaning no one can hear, smell, see, or feel me. Plus, if I tried to strangle him, my hands would just go right through him.

I floated behind Siddiqis as he unlocked the door and walked out. We stepped out into a long hallway, and after walking up a couple of stairs, he threw open a door that lead to the back of the library and stepped through, with me trailing behind him. It was the next day, and the morning breeze was light and soothing, though it just went right through me. I followed Siddiqis to his black Honda and saw him lay my body across the backseat and then slid into the driver's seat. Clearly not trusting him with my body, I went into the Honda and sat beside my body. I looked eerily peaceful, and I shuddered.

It took about five minutes to get to the castle, and when we got there, I saw there were no guards at the front. Siddiqis stopped the car and then opened the back door to retrieve my cold body. I slipped out of the car right before he locked it and then followed closely behind him. He was at the door and kicked it opened. I followed him in and saw a crowd of people running to Siddiqis, who was putting on a show of being sadden and looked like a kicked puppy. He collapsed on his knees, dramatically, and laid my body on the floor, my head on his lap. He looked at the crowd of servants with a look of despair and sorrow.

"Everybody, move!" Everyone turned and saw Aries, who was wearing a black tuxedo and he looked confused. It was when he made to the front of the crowd, he froze, a look of horror and shock on his face. He started shaking his head, moaning no, and fell to his knees beside my body. I floated beside his and sat down, knowing he couldn't see me. I saw with surprise that he was crying, clutching my hand and shielding my body from other's view, as if begging me to come back to life and protecting my body from any more harm even though I was already gone. I knew why he was so sad. I looked exactly like his dead wife, and seeing me dead was like seeing Luna die all over again. He had lost yet another woman, both dear to his heart. He sobbed and sobbed, not caring that several servants stared in shock at the sight of their king crying like a child.

"What's going on?" a strong male, yet familiar, voice called from outside the crowd, behind Aries and I. Everybody turned to see Darq, Gustav, Boota, and Bonzai, all confused.

I groaned to myself, knowing that the worst was at hand.

CHAPTER 29

Time to Mourn

REALIZING SOMETHING BAD had happened, they pushed through the crowd, and when the four saw Aries crying, they looked in confusion. "Father, what's wrong?" Gustav asked in a hard, yet soothing tone, trying to peer at what his father was crying about.

Aries sobbed even more as he moved over a little, still holding my hand, so they could see why he was crying. "She's gone," he sobbed. He continued to cry even harder.

The four of them looked and then froze at the sight of my dead body. Everyone was silent, except for the sobs of Aries.

Then Boota let out a blood-curling scream as it registered in her head the dead body was I. She fell to her knees, her face buried in her small hands, and she cried as well. The three brothers stood there, staring at my body.

A second later Bonzai stumbled back, realizing whom the dead body belonged to, and fell backward. It was Gustav that caught him as he fell, Bonzai's weight dragged them both down to the ground, and several servants scurried back as they landed on the floor.

I stared, astonished, at the two as Gustav held his brother, forcing Bonzai to look away from my body. "Don't look, brother. It's okay. Everything will be fine," he said, trying to soothe his little brother whose face was buried in his older brother's chest like a child as he sobbed. I saw, with shock, that silent tears ran down Gustav's face, though he tried looking brave, as he muttered soothing words to Bonzai.

Darq knelt down beside Boota, who was crying so hard she started hiccupping, and held her in his arms, aware that his father was there but he didn't care. Boota was in pain and he cared for her more than anything. He spoke to her in a soothing tone, assuring her everything would be all right, though he looked shaken up as well. I knew he had to be strong because he was the oldest and Gustav had to be stronger because he had a hard appearance, but both looked like they couldn't bear the sight of their loved ones being hurt; in Darq's case it was Boota crying and in Gustav's case, it was my body being still and I not breathing. I just sat there, watching the people I loved cry their hearts out. I continued to stare at the sight.

Finally, Aries stopped crying and turned to face the crowd of servants, still clutching my dead, cold, pale hand. "Go get the death angel. Now," he ordered them in a hard tone, and they all split up, looking for Angela. Aries, then, turned his attention to his eldest son and his once sadden face turned into a look of confusion. "Darq, what are you doing?"

Pulling away from Darq's embrace after realizing his father saw what he had done, Boota stood up quickly, and her cheeks went beat red and her eyes wide with fear and horror. "Forgive m-me, L-Lord Aries. I-I'll be g-going n-now!" she stuttered, and then she ran up the stairs, her head down in shame.

Darq looked red as well, though he also looked annoyed at his father for breaking the embrace. "Father, I can explain – "

"No time for that, now. We can talk later. Right now, Kyra is important." He turned to look at a sad Siddiqis, who still was playing the kicked puppy act. "What happened, Siddiqis?"

Siddiqis peered at Aries, his face full of sorrow. "I was going to train with the boys after Kyra had left, when I felt a sharp pain in my back, as if something had sliced through my spine and through my stomach. I realized that something bad had happened to Rumblen, so I wanted to go after her. But I knew if I told the boys, they'd try to come and save her and end up getting killed. I had no choice but to tie them up and put them in the supply's closet." He looked briefly at Gustav and Bonzai, both scowling at him. "Sorry about that, by the way." He turned back to Aries. "As I was saying, I drove to the Xercus library and saw a witch and her henchman guarding the front door. I knew those two were up to no good. So I ran around to the back and entered the building to find Rumblen in a prison cell located in the library's basement, with her hands tied behind her back. I broke into the room and untied her, but that wasn't the biggest problem. She was badly injured and she told me that the witch had her henchman torture her till death. Rumblen was still healing, but she was stabbed in the heart with an enchanted dagger that ended her life. She died after a minute in my arms." Siddiqis had tears streaming down his face, and he was looking at Aries in dismay. "I brought her here to be buried properly. I know that she would have wanted to be buried with her family. I won't be at the funeral because I will track down the witch and her henchman and kill them the way they killed our dear Rumblen." He leaned his head down and kissed my forehead, and I jumped up to kick him in the stomach, but my foot passed through his body. With a groan of frustration, I plopped back down next to Darq.

"Hail and farewell, my dear Kyra Rumblen Count," he whispered. He laid my head on the ground and stood up. He then walked to the front doors and walked out of the castle. Even though I wanted to follow him, I stayed with my body.

"I'm here! I'm here!" a familiar voice called. We all looked up. Angela came running down the stairs, looking distressed. She was wearing classic gear, as if ready to go to war, and her hair was held in a high ponytail. Her ivy green eyes flashed as she stopped in front of my still body. Her eyes widened. "Oh god," she gasped, a hand splayed across her chest. "I don't believe it. No, no, no. This is not right," she whispered and started shaking her head.

Aries looked up at her, confused and sad. "What do you mean?"

Angela looked down at him, her eyes showing how shocked she was. "This wasn't supposed to happen. Kyra was destined to save us. She was not destined to die. The prophecy said nothing of this," she whispered, this time louder for everybody to hear slightly.

Aries continued to push on. "Angela, what's the present prophecy?"

Angela stared at my body now, addressing everyone. "*The hybrid to break a curse bestowed by the first man shall become the Chosen Hybrid and will defeat all evil to protect the world*." She spoke in a solemn voice, a grave and analyzing look on her face. I was shocked. I knew I was a powerful hybrid, but not the Chosen Hybrid. The Chosen Hybrid was a rare legend of a hybrid that was destined for greatness. I was dead, so it didn't make any sense.

"How do you know what she's destined to do? Why should we trust your words?" Gustav questioned, eyeing Angela.

She shot him a look. "I'm a death angel. I know who dies and who doesn't. I suggest you be careful, angel of darkness. I can't say if you'll die, but I can say that I'm more powerful than you think." She looked so close to strangling Gustav, and as if sensing that, Gustav shot her an apologetic look. Angela rolled her eyes and stared at my dead pale body and shivered. "Why did you guys summon me here? I may like a good bloodshed but I don't like seeing people I like dead."

Aries stared up at her. "You're a death angel, correct?"

"Yes. Yes, I am." Angela had a smug look on her face, but her eyes showed that she was uncertain on what Aries wanted her to do.

"Revive Kyra then."

Silence rang throughout the castle as Angela's face darkened.

"No," she said simply, but I knew that one word had a huge impact behind its meaning. I, myself, also was stunned.

"What?" Aries was shocked. So was his son.

Angela's eyes flashed. "No. I will not bring Kyra back to life."

CHAPTER 30

Confessions

ARIES AND HIS three sons stared up at Angela in disbelief. "What do you mean you won't bring her back to life? Are you crazy?" Gustav demanded, as he rose to his feet to stand in front of Angela, their faces inches apart.

Angela raised her chin at Gustav, not stepping back even though I could tell she hated him being so close. "I meant I can't bring her back to life."

"Why can't you?" Gustav pushed on, his blue eyes cutting through Angela's.

"I can't bring her back because I can't," she said calmly.

This made Gustav angry. He grabbed Angela by her jacket collar and drew her toward him. He stared at her in rage, their faces closer than before. "That's not good enough for me. Give me a better answer." His voice was icy cold, and everyone stared at the scene, knowing that Gustav was treading in dangerous water.

Angela's eyes flashed, and I knew she was trying not to strangle him and trying to keep her rage down. Still, she kept a calm face. "Let go of me, angel of darkness," she commanded each word precisely in a low tone that dripped with venom.

"Answer me, and I'll consider," he challenged, and I knew that he was pushing Angela too far.

"You're making a mistake that you will for sure regret, angel of darkness. You don't want to make a death angel angry," she warned him calmly, though her tone assured him she wasn't kidding.

Gustav's eyes flashed but he released her jacket. He stared at her in disgust. "What kind of a friend are you? You won't even bring her back to life!" he shouted, and I saw Bonzai flinch at the sound.

"Stop. Just stop," Angela commanded, though her voice shook slightly, and I suddenly knew what she was trying to hide. She looked down, trying to calm herself.

"Give me one good reason why you won't!"

That made her burst. Angela's head shot up, and Gustav took a step back. Her eyes were a bright green, showing that she was angry. "I can't! I would, but I seriously can't bring her back to us!" she shouted, causing the lights to flicker for a minute. Everyone went silent.

Darq was the next to speak. "Angela, please. Tell us why you cannot." He spoke in a calm voice, assuring her that he didn't want to push her.

Angela stared hard at Darq and then sighed, giving up. She looked at my body as she spoke in a quiet voice. "Do you know what death angels can do?"

"They can revive anything that's dead and can kill anything," Gustav said, annoyed.

"That's wrong," she said, still staring at my body, ignoring Gustav's stunned expression. "I can only revive any *pure soul.* Kyra isn't a pure soul. Even though she may have been the nicest and kindest demonic hybrid, she was still a demonic hybrid. She was the daughter of Lilith, the mother of all demons, and a kind vamp. Demon blood coursed through her veins. She may have broken her mother's curse and had angelic qualities, but she was a full hybrid, and a powerful one at that. I can't bring her back even if I wanted to. I'm not that powerful. I'm sorry." She looked down in shame; admitting she wasn't the most powerful death angel was tough for her.

They were silent and I just stayed there next to my body, watching them. It was Bonzai who broke the silence. "What do we do now?" His green eyes were wide and he looked lost.

Aries looked at his eldest son. "Darq, you and Gustav will carry Kyra's body to her room. We must make arrangements for a casket. Bonzai, you need to go tell the servants that they will be dismissed of their duties for today. I think we all need time to think things over. Now if you may need me, I'll be in the training room." After squeezing my pale hand, affectingly, he stood and walked to the training room, his footsteps echoed through the foyer. We all just stayed there, and then, without saying a word, Angela ran up the stairs and disappeared through a door at the top of the stairs. We were all silent.

It was Darq who broke the silence. "I can't believe she's actually gone." He walked over to my body and sat down beside me.

Bonzai got up, Gustav helping him stand, and both brothers walked to their eldest brother's side and sat beside him; Darq next to Gustav, Gustav next to Bonzai. I got up to sit across form them on the other side of my body. They stared at my dead body in silence.

"We must avenge Kyra." Gustav eyes flashed with rage and vengeance.

"For once in my life, I actually agree with you," Bonzai replied, causing Gustav to look at his younger brother with pride and surprise.

"I would like to strangle who did this as well, but now is not the time to talk of revenge," Darq said, his tone deep and full of wisdom. "Today, we mourn."

The two nodded, though Gustav's eyes flashed in protest.

Then, Gustav and Darq got up and Bonzai stood as well to go to the servant's quarters, his face was blank. Gustav picked me up and held me in his arms, and I knew he didn't want anybody else to touch me. Darq, okay with Gustav's choice, led the way up the stairs, and I followed the boys all the way back to my room. They opened the door and I realized that someone had unlocked it before. Darq held the door open for Gustav and then he closed the door behind them. Gustav carried my body to my bed and placed me down gently, so that my head was resting on the pillows, and he drew the blankets over my cold, lifeless body. I knew he was trying to draw heat to my body, but it was no use. The dead can't feel heat. I felt empty, like a big piece of me was missing.

"I'll leave you some time with Kyra. After, come to the training room so we could spar," Darq said and with that he closed the door behind him, leaving Gustav, my body, and I alone in the room. I floated to the opposite side of the bed and peered at Gustav. Even in grief, he had that bad-boy charm, which I adored. I then realized how attractive he was. His dark hair covered his forehead and his muscular body had my eyes lingering there. His eyes were like crystals, icy and beautiful. It was so easy to get yourself caught in his gaze. I couldn't help but think, *Damn, he's sexy.*

He was kneeling beside my bed, staring at my body with love and despair. "Oh, Kyra. Why have you left me?" he whispered. "I don't understand why you had to die. I love you so much. Losing you is like losing my mother again. Please come back to me. Please come back. Please, please, please," he begged, tears streamed down his face. "I can't stand seeing your body so lifeless. I want to hear you laugh. I want to see you smile. If I could talk to you one last time, I'd savor it forever like savoring the stars in the night before they disappear and return after a full day. Even a second would relieve me of this pain. I love you, Kyra Rumblen Count. I love you." He sobbed, his face buried in the sheets beside my body and his shoulders shook. I tried to imagine his love coursing through me, but all I felt was emptiness. We were silent.

That's when I heard it: the beating of a heart. I looked around, frantically, wondering who was with us. No one was there. I pressed a hand to my soul's chest and felt nothing. I pressed a hand to my own body's chest and my hand slipped through my chest. I hastily pulled back my hand. Then, I closed my eyes, and using my bat's sonar, I tracked the sound of a beating heart . . . all the way to Gustav.

CHAPTER 31

Miracles

I GASPED, IN surprise and happiness. *His heart is beating! The curse has been broken!* I realized, cheering to myself. I peered at Gustav with pure delight and saw he felt it too.

He placed a hand over his heart and closed his eyes. After a second or two, he gasped and his eyes shot open, wide with surprise. He peered down at his chest, which was rising up and down. He gasped again this time savoring the air full his lungs, and for the first time, he felt the wonder of breathing to live. "I'm alive. My heart is beating." He looked at my body and smiled radiantly. "You broke my curse. This was your gift to me, was it not? I guess I can now say that I love you with my now beating whole heart, Rumblen."

I froze at the sound of my middle name, not in terror of hearing my birth name, but because the one I loved actually used the name with a purpose. *He said my middle name. With love. He loves me. I broke the curse,* I realized, thoughts swirling in my head. I was happy he used my name. He deserved to call me whatever he wanted only because he truly loved me, and I loved him. I trusted him.

"It was not her gift to you, angel of darkness," a sweet voice said, the sound echoed in the room. Gustav whirled around to find a woman standing in front of him. She had glowing pearl white skin and golden waves that went over her shoulders. Her eyes were a mesmerizing gold that laughed of sunshine and joy. I knew right away what this woman was. She was an angel. An angel of life. She smiled at his shocked expression. "It was no gift. Kyra Rumblen Count broke the curse my sister had bestowed upon you since your birth: *'For the first born shall not be a joy, but a burden that will cause havoc among every soul unless true love is found.'* I have restored your heartbeat, angel of darkness, and now I will grant you one wish, for now you have found true love. The one thing your heart desires is yours."

Gustav peered at the woman, his gaze set, and I knew he already knew what he wanted. "Rumblen. I would like Rumblen back."

The woman grinned, playfully, and then laughed. "I should have known. She was the one who broke the curse. And you must be very fond of her to ask for such a wish. Very well. I shall grant you the kiss of life."

"I beg your pardon? It is not I that needs the kiss of life. It is Rumblen!" Gustav backed up a step and was stopped by the bed.

The angel laughed and the sunshine grew brighter. "My dear angel of darkness, I meant I shall bestow upon you the *power* to bring back your beloved with a single kiss. But you only get one kiss and then the power is gone from you." She then took Gustav's hand and muttered words in the angelic language, and I saw the power, a blue orb, as it traveled up Gustav's arm and to his lips. Then the angel withdrew her hand and smiled. "There. May the angels bless you both." And with that, she disappeared into thin air.

Gustav turned back to my body and took in a breath, and I knew he was praying the angel was right about the kiss. He then lowered his face to mine and kissed me on the lips. It was the best kiss I had experienced because it filled me with life. Literally.

Instantly, I felt energy course through my soul and I felt myself being drawn back to my body. As I entered my body, I was thrown into a pit of light, and then it was gone in a second. I felt my heart start to beat and I heaved in a breath of air through my mouth and exhaled, slowly, with a gasp. That's when I opened my eyes.

Gustav gasped and fell on to the ground, in shock. I hauled in another breath, this time savoring the feeling of air in my system once again, and then let out the breath in a shaky, happy sigh. I slowly sat up, wincing at the pain, and saw that I was fully healed up, just sore. I peered down at Gustav who was staring at me as if I were an angel. We stayed there for a second, soaking in each other's love and shock.

Finally, I grinned at him. "I never knew you were so poetic. Maybe we should call you the Poetic Gustav, like how the servants call Darq the Artistic Darq." I laughed at the thought and at his relieved expression, as if he was relieved that I still had the energy to crack a funny comment at a time like that. It felt good to be back.

Gustav jumped to his feet and embraced me into a long hug, and though I felt sore, I ignored the pain for the pleasure of the moment. I felt the beating of his heart and realized he was crying tears of joy. "I thought you were gone. I thought I lost you too." He sobbed, his voice filling me with joy and delight.

"I would never leave you alone, my dear Gustav," I assured him, tears filled in my eyes. I realized I sounded like Siddiqis when I saved him from turning full evil, but I pushed the thought out of my head, knowing that I didn't stop the evil from controlling him. Plus, I wanted to savor that moment. All I knew was that I wanted to embrace the moment I came back to life.

Gustav broke the embrace, his icy blue eyes shone with love, and he smiled. "Even if you wanted to leave me, I wouldn't have let you. And if you try to leave me again, I'll tie you to me if I have to."

I giggled and then realized something. "Oh shoot, everybody thinks I'm dead."

Gustav's expression turned playful. "Should we prank my father into thinking your ghost is haunting him?"

I thought of that and then dismissed it with a laugh. "As much as I would like to scare your father to death, we can't. We have to tell them I'm alive before your father arranges a casket for me."

Gustav nodded. "Should I call Siddiqis and tell him – "

"No! Don't tell Siddiqis!" I interrupted quickly. Seeing Gustav's shocked and questioning expression, I sighed. "Siddiqis isn't as innocent as we thought."

Gustav's eyes flashed. "I knew it! He mistreated you, didn't he? That little – "

"No," I interrupted again, "Siddiqis and I may have had a history together before, but this is different. Something sinister." I retold Gustav everything that happened, what really happened, and Siddiqis's plan.

After explaining everything, Gustav jumped to his feet, looking ready to kill. "Now, I'm going to really kill that sly weasel." He cracked his knuckles for effect, but I just laughed. He really was like his father: stubborn, a showoff, tough, and cute in a dangerously sexy way.

CHAPTER 32

Old and New at the Same Time

WHEN I GOT off the bed, I felt my legs give away, but Gustav was there to catch me. I realized, with a groan, that it was back to baby steps for me. After thirty minutes, I was able to walk again because of constant cheering and pressure from Gustav and I waltzed into the bathroom, my war gear in tow. I striped off the bloody dress and took a hot shower to wash off the dried blood from my body. Soon, I was dressed head to toe in full war gear: black vest topped with a black leather jacket, black leather thighs and combat boots. I then emerged out of the bathroom to see Gustav sitting on the bed. When he saw me, he stared, dazed, and I knew it was because I looked like a younger version of his mother, yet tougher. I tied my hair into a ponytail and put on my weapons belt. I slipped my daggers and knives into their slots and slipped my sword into its sheath. I stood back and peered at my reflection in the mirror and stepped back with a gasp as I saw one of my eyes were a gold and the other a stormy gray. I heard Gustav gasp as well and then I realized that since I died with these eyes, these would be my new permanent eyes. I decided to throw on some shades, so I wouldn't alarm the servants. Though that didn't mean I wouldn't have any fun scaring people.

I turned and smiled at Gustav, assuring him it was just my real eyes, and he was already off the bed and heading for the door. Right before he opened the door, he paused. Then, he turned and embraced me into a loving, quick kiss. It lasted for a minute and then we broke away. I grinned. "The power in the kiss only works once. Sorry pal, I'm not feeling anymore alive. I'm still a vamp."

He chuckled. "Leave it to you to break the moment and bring me back to reality," and then he held the door open for me. We stepped out into the hallway and walked to the stairs.

When we got to the top of the staircase, I stopped Gustav with a grin. "Let me show you how to really make an entrance. I need to make sure I'm not rusty from dying." And with that, I flew over the top railing and dropped down, and I heard Gustav swear. I landed softly on my feet, crouching, and stood up to find several servants staring at me in horror and shock. I lowered my shades, so they could see my eyes, and peered at the stunned and terrified servants. I grinned at them and waved to them. "I'm back," I sang in a ghostly and sinister, yet amusing, voice.

They all looked at each other and then went running up the stairs, opposite of the one I leapt off of, terrified of me. I couldn't help but chuckle.

Gustav laughed from the top of the stairs and then, leapt from the top, flipped in the air twice, and landed as silent as a cat on the bottom, on his feet. He bowed, grinning.

I shook my head, scowling at him with my eyes narrowed, as I pushed my shades up to my eyes. "Show off."

He laughed and then motioned for me to follow him to the training room. We jogged down the hallway, and soon, we were standing in front of the training room door. Gustav peered at me, grinning. "I still can't believe you're alive, Rumblen."

A burst of energy surged through me at the sound of my name. I winked at him, grinning. "C'mon. Let's go inside and surprise your father."

He nodded and we threw open the doors. The doors closed behind us, just as a dagger lodged into the wall beside Gustav's head. He looked at the dagger, then at me, wide eyed, and then he looked at the person who threw it.

Aries stood in the middle of the room, hands on his hips, looking annoyed. It was clear he hadn't noticed me. "Gustav, how many times have I told you not to enter without – " He paused in mid-sentence when he saw me. Aries was in his training gear and I saw that he wasn't alone. Darq was there, also in training gear, stretching, and when he saw us, he froze half way into the splits and jumped to his feet. We were all silent and still, staring at each other.

Finally, Gustav and I stepped out of the shadows and deeper into the room, closer to Aries. We stopped when we were a couple of steps away from Aries and Darq. I looked at the two and then laid my gaze on Aries, who was pale as if he had seen a ghost.

I grinned at him. "By your expression, I'm guessing you think I'm haunting you. But I can assure you – "

I was cut off when Aries swooped me into a long embrace. I may have been slightly sore, but I ignored it for the sake of the moment. I hugged him back and took in his body heat. He pulled back after a minute, taking me by the shoulders, and looked at me, really looked at me. He frowned. "Why are you wearing shades? The lights aren't that bright."

I heaved in a breath. "Just don't freak out." I saw his bewildered expression and took off my shades. My eyes flashed. I felt strangely insecure with the shades off, and I tried not to wince at the lights. Of course, I kept my eyes closed for too long so my eyes were still adjusting to the lighting.

Aries gasped and then lifted a hand to my cheek, his eyes searching for an explanation. "What happened?"

I exhaled with a sigh, happy he wasn't freaking out. "It's nothing. This is my hybrid mark and I died with it showing. So these are my new permanent eyes. You'll have to get use to it." I shrugged.

Darq came up to me and swooped me into a hug that last for a few seconds and he smiled. "I'm glad you're back. Plus, I like your eyes how they are now. They really fit you." He smiled, though I knew he was slightly uncomfortable. I couldn't blame him. My hybrid mark was a peculiar one and my gaze held more control than before. I put my shades back on and instantly felt more secure, and a wave of relief washed over my eyes.

Aries then exhaled, and I knew it was because he thought it was something too serious. "I'll call Siddiqis and tell him – "

"No!" Gustav and I shouted at the same time.

Aries and Darq flinched at the sound. Aries stared at us with questioning eyes and I knew he was confused.

I sighed. "You can't trust him." I then launched into a full explanation of what really happened and Siddiqis's plan to free the demons and attack the kingdoms, starting with Xercus.

Aries swore under his breath. "I should have known. We must assemble the soldiers." He turned to his eldest son. "Go get the soldiers and tell them to get ready for war. And find your brother. He must be in the servant's quarters."

Darq nodded and then ran out the door, shutting it behind him.

Aries turned to face me, his expression dead serious. "You and Gustav should head out to the foyer, but first, grab whatever you need."

I nodded and then, turned and walked with Gustav. We were about to go, when I turned back to face Aries. "Do you mind if I go back to the Mortal Portal to gather my army, so we could have more enforcement?"

Aries looked shocked and then he shook his head, smiling. "No, that would be perfect! Go get whatever you need and head to the Mortal Portal. Gustav will go with you and gather your best troops. Be careful." He turned away to gather weapons he needed, and I took that as a cue to leave the room, and I followed Gustav to the front.

Gustav stopped at the bottom of the stairs and turned to face me. He gazed at me with loving eyes. “I need to go to my room to get my special weapons. You coming?”

I nodded and we ran up the stairs and down the hall opposite of where my room was. We passed several doors, and finally, Gustav stopped at one door that said, *Gustav's Room.* He opened the door and we stepped in, the door closed behind us. Gustav's room was like mine, though weapons were everywhere. Plus, dirty laundry was all over the floor and I realized that I was gapping at the scene as if I had just seen Godzilla right in front of me. Actually, I'm pretty sure Godzilla would have been gapping at the scene as well.

Gustav saw my expression and he laughed. “Welcome to a real man's room.” He gestured around grandly and then went to work trying to free a dagger for a wall.

I gaped. “You call this a room? I call this a pit of despair.”

He laughed as he hooked on his weapons belt to his hips and began slotting in dagger and knives, each one different and unique. He then attached his sword into its sheath and I knew by the way he treated it carefully as if it were glass, it was a special sword crafted for him. He didn't look up as he spoke. “My mother made me this sword right before the war that ended her life.” He closed his eyes and I knew he was thinking about Luna. Finally, he opened his eyes and walked over to me. He caressed my cheek with the back of his right hand. “Are you sure you can fight, Rumblen? You've just risen from the dead.” He spoke in a caring voice and I saw the fear of losing me again in his icy blue eyes.

I reached for his left hand and clutched it to my heart. “If you hadn't noticed, I feel fine and stronger than before. I'm not sore anymore and I'm ready to fight.” I kissed him on the lips softly. It sent shivers of delight up my arms and I knew he wanted more, but I held off. “Now, we've got to head out to the Mortal Portal and gather up my troops.” And with that we were out of his room and out the castle's front door. We climbed into Gustav's red Jeep and headed off to my kingdom. I was heading back home after all.

CHAPTER 33

Back for Help

AFTER ABOUT THIRTY minutes of Gustav's crazy driving, we finally arrived to the front of my castle alive thankfully. It looked the same as it was when I left and I realized that I never expected to come back in full war gear to recruit soldiers. I was holding the seatbelt so tightly I ripped it from the fear I was going to die and I was breathing hard. Gustav peered at me and then brought his focus back to the front of the car as he pulled into the front, where I met Bonzai for the first time and where Gustav found out I was going to marry him or one of his brothers and had fainted. I pushed the memories aside and focused on the task ahead. Finally, we pulled to a stop, missing the statue of my mother and father by an inch. I scowled at him. "You know, I may have died three times now, but that doesn't mean I want to die a *fourth* time! God, you are never driving again! I'd rather walk back than get back into this red metal deathtrap!" I threw the thrown up seatbelt bits onto the Jeep's floor.

He gave me an astonished look. "C'mon, I'm not that bad at driving, am I?" We climbed out of the Jeep and made our way up the front steps.

"You almost killed us!" I argued.

"But we lived," he pointed out.

"We almost died!"

"At least I didn't wreck anything."

"You crashed into a barn, knocked over the wheat, trampled over dozens of crops, and ran over several chickens!" I rebutted at him.

"So what? At least no one got hurt!"

"Wish we could say that about the chickens!"

"No one's going to miss a couple of chickens!"

"Oh, heavens! You're so stubborn!" I threw my hands in the air in frustration and defeat.

"Yes, I am. It's funny how you know that and yet, you still try to argue with me." He flashed me a grin and I stuck my tongue out at him, causing him to laugh. We sound like an old aged couple and I enjoyed arguing with him. It made him grin more often and Gustav grinning was a beautiful sight. His grin was kind of like a smirk, an incredibly sexy smirk.

Finally, we stood in front of the doors of my castle. Gustav looked at me and I knew I had to be the one who opened the door because to open the door, we had to do an eye scan for security reasons. I lowered my shades down the bridge of my nose and leveled both of my eyes to the scanner. It quickly scanned my eyes and the light went from red to green, signaling us entry, and I slid my shades back up to my eyes. I heaved in a breath, taking in the scent of my old home, and exhaled as I opened the doors. The inside looked the same, as always, which was that it looked like the Xercus castle, and it appeared that nothing out of the ordinary was happening. I took in another breath and took a step inside the castle. Nothing happened. I looked back at Gustav and motioned for him to follow me in. We walked in and clearly annoyed that nobody heard us enter, Gustav slammed the door shut behind us. I shot him a scowl and waited for someone to come.

Finally, someone came running down the grand stairs and I instantly knew whom it was. "Who's there?" Arwin Vansiv called as she ran down the stairs to see us. I felt a wave of relief wash over me, as I peered at my old friend through the tinted lens of the shades. Arwin hadn't changed a bit of course, though I felt bad when I saw dark circles shadowing under her and I knew she hadn't had much sleep. It's hard ruling a country all by yourself, but I knew she was strong enough to take on such a task. It wasn't like taking care of a child; it was like taking care of dozens of children. I was so happy to see her again.

When she got closer, she gasped and I realized she hadn't seen me, but she had seen Gustav. Her brown eyes widened, in shock, and she pointed a shaky finger at him. "*You?* How dare you come here? And how did you get past the eye scanner? You know what your father has done to us and you think we will forgive you for his mistakes? You better get out of here before I make you get out!" Oh boy. She wasn't scared. She was angry, and an angry unicorn was a scary unicorn.

Gustav threw me a confused look and looked back at a steaming Arwin. He held his hands in front of him, as if to show her he wasn't a threat. "Please. I didn't come here for trouble. I'm – "

"Oh please! I know all about you, angel of darkness! You killed many of our loved ones! Leave now or face the con – "

"Oh, I don't think you want me to leave." He took a step toward her and she stepped back.

"Get out of here!" she shouted, and I saw her eyes were turning red. She was getting angry, and I knew that it wasn't a good sign.

Instantly, I took off my shades, allowing Arwin to see my eyes. "Arwin!" I shouted to get her attention.

She turned to me, noticing me for the first time and her eyes widened.

I smiled. "I know Gustav can be a little intimidating, but he's good. You can trust him. When have I ever let you down?"

She raised a hand up to her mouth, astonished by the sight of me. "*Kyra? Kyra Rumblen Count?*" She shook her head in disbelief, and I knew she was stunned.

I took a step toward her and grinned. "That's me."

She moved like lightning, swooping me into a long embrace. I hugged her back, and I felt hot tears run down my cheeks. I missed her so much. She was like another sister to me. She was crying too, tears of joy sprung out of her eyes. "I thought I was never going to see you again! I'm so happy you're back!" She broke the embrace and looked from Gustav to me and then, gasped. "Is he *the one*?" By the way she said "the one," I blushed, knowing instantly what she was talking about.

I grinned at her and then whispered in her ear. "Maybe."

She squealed like a child who had just gotten a lollipop and looked at Gustav, apologetic. "Sorry about what I said before. My bad," she apologized and Gustav nodded, accepting her apology. Her eyes went back to their warm brown color and I let out a relieved sigh. She turned back to me, beaming. "I'm so glad you're back! I'll get your room key and – "

"Um, I'm not back to stay," I interrupted and earned confused look from her. "Arwin, has Siddiqis visited the castle while I was gone?"

She looked taken back by the question. "No, he hasn't. Why?"

I looked her in the eye, a serious look on my face. "We've got a big problem." I retold everything that happened to me when I was going to the library, Siddiqis's plan, how Siddiqis killed me, how he lied to everyone saying he found me dead, and how Gustav brought me back to life.

Arwin listened attentively, and when I finished talking, she was silent. Finally, she let out a shaky breath. "I can't believe it. Siddiqis has always been there for us, and now he's gone crazy!"

Because of me, I thought and then I pushed the thought off a cliff inside of my mind. "We need to send all of our troops to Xercus, to help them against the demons. Gather them all and tell them to get in gear and meet me here," I told Arwin and she nodded, already running up the staircase and I knew she was going to the soldier's quarters.

When she disappeared, I turned to face Gustav and swore under my breath. He snuck up behind me and was peering down at me, catching my arms as if to steady me or to hold me there. He lowered his mouth onto mine and I felt him melt into my system. Our systems collided; we merged together, became as one. I felt his pain, his sorrow, his love, and I moaned in pleasure. We broke apart, gasping for air and stared at each other, as if communicating through our love. I grinned at him. "What do you think Arwin would say if she saw us just right now?"

"She would probably kick me all the way back to Xercus." He took a moment to imagine that and then broke off into a laugh so contagious I started laughing as well. Leave it to Gustav to make me laugh at a time like that.

We stopped laughing only when the troops arrived, full in war gear, and they stared at me, shocked at seeing their princess back in full war gear as well. They gasped when they saw Gustav next to me.

Gustav cleared his throat. "Hello, gentlemen. I don't believe we have met properly. I am Gustav Deatheye, son of Luna and Aries Deatheye." He gave them a salute and his best-selling grin while I tried not to laugh.

I looked at my troops all in the eye, dead serious. "I have come back to ask of your assistance. Xercus is going to be at battle with an army of demons. What you must remember is that our old friend Siddiqis Starburn is leading this army of demons. He is not to be trusted. We must help Xercus, for if they are to be vanquished, we are next. This will be a good way for us to finally work side by side and lead into victory together. Many lives will be lost and only the brave will live. I thank you all for your bravery and may Heaven be on our side and lead us to victory." They all stared at me and I realized that I had just recited what my mother said to them before her last battle. I then turned to Gustav, who was staring at me with admiration and opened the door as we led the army outside and the troop climbed into their Jeeps. Of course, I had to get into Gustav's Jeep again and we trailed behind in his Jeep to make sure we weren't being followed. This time he drove much safer.

He clutched my hand with one hand and stirred with the other. He looked over at me, concerned. "Are you sure you can fight?" he asked for the fifth time since we had gotten into the Jeep.

I looked at him and smiled. "I want to fight. Plus, I feel like putting Siddiqis's head on a stick." I slipped my shades back on.

He chuckled. "Don't we all?" He squeezed my hand, affectionately and I turned away to look out the window. I realized that was it. That was the day I was going to gain something and lose something. I knew that battle would be the biggest one I would ever been in and that I might have been leading my troops into a suicide mission. But as long as Gustav was with me, I knew I was going to be okay. We were all going to be okay. And I just couldn't wait to see the expression on Siddiqis's face when he saw that I was alive and going to end his life just like he had to mine.

CHAPTER 34

Bloodshed

WHEN WE PULLED up to the front of the castle, all I heard were screams. We all jumped out of our Jeeps and ran to the back of the castle. The back of the castle was a huge battlefield and I barely saw the Lake of Tears, which was more than a mile away. First thing I saw when we got to the field was blood, staining the grass. It was chaos. Demons ran amok, fighting the Xercus soldiers. I wasn't expecting to see so many demons. They outnumbered the Xercus army by two hundred, and I knew that our army wouldn't help the odds of winning. I couldn't find Aries, Darq, or Bonzai in the crowd of soldiers, and I hoped they weren't one of the bodies that lay bloody on the ground. And I prayed that Boota wasn't fighting in the battle.

I turned to face my men and nodded. Then, I felt a hand slip into mine. I looked to my left to see Gustav looking at me, and I felt a boost of courage surge through me. I gave him a reassuring squeeze and he nodded, his gaze full serious and on me. I turned to face the field and took in the metallic smell, my fangs begging to be let out to taste some blood but I kept them in. I yelled out our battle cry, my mother's name, and we all sprang into action. We charged into the fight, taking the demons by surprise. Several of my men ran to the Xercus soldiers that weren't doing so well and fought by their side, ignoring their harsh past with each other. I ran into the fight with Gustav trailing behind me, guarding my back and pulled out a dagger. I sliced the head off of a slimy, fleshy demon that had one eye and a tentacle and I enjoyed the sound of the dagger slicing through the creature's flesh and the sickening thump of its head hitting the ground. I turned to Gustav and saw he was struggling with a short blue demon that was clawing at him with long sharp talons. I slid on my knees toward the two, and as I passed Gustav and the demon, I neatly sank my blade into the demon's neck and left it there. The demon shook and then turned to ashes. I got up and then picked up my dagger from the pile of demon ashes. I looked around and saw my troops were working with the Xercus troops as one, and I felt pride bubble inside me. I realized one person was MIA: Siddiqis.

I turned to Gustav, who read my mind. He gave me a quick kiss and stared at me, serious and lovingly. "Go get him, but be careful. I'm going to find Bonzai and tell him you're alive, though I'm pretty sure Darq told him. Good luck, Rumblen." He stroked my cheek and I could tell he was scared about both of us.

I grinned at him. "Don't worry. I was born for this, remember?"

He nodded and hugged me. "Good luck, Chosen Hybrid." He released me after a minute and then ran into a crowd for demons that weren't going down easy. He slit several necks of demons and I knew he enjoyed the sound of demons dying just as much as I did. I ran through the field, searching for my old friend. I slit the necks of the demons that dared to fight me and each one fell down, dead. I looked around, looking for any sign of my friends, and I took off my shades to get a better look. I looked to my right and saw Aries fighting off a herd of horned green demons, as he stabbed them all. He looked dead serious and he really was scary when he had that crazy look in his black eyes. I looked to my left and saw Angela fighting a tall three-headed demon. She was intimidating it by running around it with super speed, and when she was behind it, she slit off its legs in one swipe. It went down with a roar, and Angela took it as the opportunity to slice off its middle head and the demon crumpled to the ground. Angela looked up and saw me, shooting me a scary grin, and I knew killing demons was Angela's favorite hobby. I flashed her a grin as well and kept going. I couldn't find Darq or Bonzai and I decided that they must have been fighting beside each other. As I ran, I felt a sting in my leg and I cried out in shock and pain. I whirled around to see a small demon shaped as a scorpion and realized the fool had stung me. Fortunately, poison didn't affect me because normal poison had no affect against me, and I snapped the demon's neck, satisfied when I heard the sickening crack and as it fell to the ground dead. I turned back around and took a knee. After cleaning my daggers with a piece of cloth I kept extra, I silenced the world around me by calming my mind. I looked back at my memories and thoughts, searching for a hint to where Siddiqis was.

After two minutes, I was about to give up in frustration and find him myself when a memory came to my mind: The Lake of Tears – the lake where Siddiqis threw me in when I drank all of the apple juice out of his juice box. I remember the look on his face when he picked me up and threw me in, the way he laughed and even the way he helped me out of the lake, threatening to let go of my hand

and drop me in again. That was the day I officially met him, besides the day I met him and his father. That was the day I really met the real Siddiqis Starburn. It had hit me that he was there. It was the perfect place because no one would think he was there.

I grinned to myself, as if I had won the lottery, and stood up. I took off running to the Lake of Tears; courage surge through me. As I ran, I pulled out two daggers from their slots and ran clutching them, one in each hand. I couldn't wait to sink the blades into Siddiqis's flesh and hear his cries of pain and defeat. *Whoa, calm down, Kyra,* I told myself. *Don't let vengeance get to your head. Killing Siddiqis will only mean getting justice. Don't let vengeance drive you.* Finally, I arrived at the Lake of Tears and stopped. It was a great body of water, not too big and not too small, and the water was enchanted with the tears of the angels. The water was a dark blue and reflected anything that peered at it, showing those who peer at themselves who they really are. I looked around and felt my heart skip a beat.

Siddiqis was on his knees with his head down, his back facing me. He was looking at his reflection, unaware he had company. I silently walked toward him, hands sweaty and threatening to drop both daggers. I remained calm, knowing that even one worried thought would set off Siddiqis. I had to approach him as if I was the hunter and he was the prey. Finally, I stopped a couple steps away from him and closed my eyes to remember all of my training. I had a fair chance of winning because I was fully healed and I took the chance to mutter words in the angelic language that enchanted my daggers and knives, but not my sword. Now, I was ready to face my old friend. I opened my eyes to see Siddiqis was now standing, his back still facing me. I slipped my shades on to hide my identity.

I was about to take another step toward him, when he spoke. "I know someone's here."

CHAPTER 35

Hello Again

I FROZE, MY foot hovering over the ground.

He chuckled. "Who is that and how stupid are you to challenge the great Siddiqis Starburn?" His voice was strong for someone who killed his old friend.

I placed my foot down beside the other. I grinned and decided to answer his question honestly to give him a scare. "I am Kyra Rumblen Count, daughter of Curtis Count and Lilith Demonheart, and I am here to deliver your death sentence, Siddiqis Starburn."

Siddiqis spun around to face me. He went pale and I knew he was slightly frightened. He killed me, and yet, there I was, standing in front of him. If I were he, I'd run into the lake. "Impossible," he whispered. He was in full war gear as well, though he was wearing a sleeveless leather jacket. He looked tough, but still I saw fear in his eyes. He didn't dare move.

I smirked. "Missed me?"

He collected himself rather quickly, more quickly than I hoped, and stared at me. "You have the voice, you've said the name perfectly, and you've got the attitude. But I still don't believe you're Kyra Rumblen Count." He looked serious, even a little angry.

I knew right on the spot what to say that would convince him. I gestured at the lake. "It's funny how I knew you were here, is it not? I mean, I was looking everywhere, and then I took a knee and remembered something." I stepped toward him.

He looked cautious, as if I were a bomb that could explode in any second if he cut the wrong wire. "What did you remember?"

I stared at him through my shades. "I remembered the day when you threw me into the lake, just because I drank all of you apple juice from your juice box. I knew that lake held something dear to you and that's how I knew you were here." I took another step.

Siddiqis was angry and stunned. "How do you know that?"

I took my shades off; I was tired of hiding behind a pair of tinted lens and my eyes flashed, wickedly. "Because that was me you threw into the lake."

He gasped and then his eyes widened. "Kyra Rumblen Count?" he whispered. I thought he was considering jumping into the lake, but he held back.

I tilted my head, smirking. "You haven't changed at all, Siddiqis Starburn. Of course, you did kill me today and I'm still here. Isn't Xercus pretty at this time of the day?" I gestured around, and it was true. It was still the afternoon and the wind was starting to pick up as the sun beamed on. Spring was the best season for battles because it wasn't too hot and it wasn't too cold. Of course, there were quite a few clouds, but no chance of those being rain clouds.

Siddiqis had his full attention on me, his eyes narrowed. "How are you still alive?"

I pouted. "I thought you were going to be happy that I was alive." I let out a big laugh, as though it was the funniest joke, and grinned. "Just joking. I know you're not happy at all. In fact, you must be pretty damn scared."

Siddiqis glared at me, his magenta eyes flashed. "Actually, I'm feeling murderous. Answer me. How are you still alive?" he asked again, his voice dripped with venom.

I smiled a little too sweetly. "I did the same thing I did when I was born. I broke a curse." I saw his confused expression and grinned. "It's clear you've forgotten that one of the Deatheye boys was cursed." I smirked.

He looked down, lost in thought, and then realization had hit him. "*For the first born shall not be a joy, but a burden that will cause havoc among every soul unless true love is found*," he muttered, reciting Gustav's curse. He looked up at me. "That was Gustav's curse, wasn't it? I should have known."

"Yes, you should've."

"Do you know who you are now?" he asked, uncertain.

I was shocked. "What am I?"

He smirked. "The Chosen Hybrid."

"Yes, I just wanted you to admit I'm the most powerful hybrid." I had a smug expression on my face.

Siddiqis huffed. "Not for long."

I ignored the last remark. Silence passed between us. I cleared my voice and raised an eyebrow. "You know the battle's on the other side of the field, right? Or are you having the demons fight your own battle?" I was trying to intimidate him and I made sure he knew that I was in charge. I raised my chin at him, challenging him with a cocky grin plastered on my face.

Surprising me, he grinned back evilly. "I was actually waiting. The demons are meant to ward off people from coming here, but if someone were able to sneak past them, I'd slaughter them my way. Of course, you're the only one who actually realized I was missing and decided to come after me." He eyed me, taking in my gear and his eyes landed on my new eyes. "I see your hybrid's mark is showing. I'm guessing it's going to be like that forever."

I shrugged. "I like my new eyes. They show who I really am."

He raised his eyebrows, amused, and smirked. "Huh. That works too. So the first time I killed you, you came back to life. Now, I think it's proper to say this ends here." His hand crept to his sword's hilt, resting there in case I decided to make the first move.

I nodded. "I guess you're right. One of us leaves alive while the other sleeps forever." I gripped my daggers tighter, calculating the distance between us.

Siddiqis grinned. "Correct, though you missed one small detail."

I narrowed my eyes at him. "And what's that?"

"I'm going to leave alive while you sleep forever." And with that, he lunged at me, hands outstretched to grab me and pull me down.

I was ready for him and moved out of the way, as he went crashing to his knees. I drove a dagger into the back of his shoulder and drew it out, enjoying the sight of his blood on my dagger. Siddiqis let out a shout of pain, maybe annoyance, and then jumped up back on his feet. His eyes blazed with rage and I knew he wasn't expecting that. "I see dying made you faster." He reached to touch his shoulder and his hand came away bloody.

I grinned, ready to attack again. "It didn't just make me fast, it made me better than before." I threw aside my two daggers to charge at him, catching him by the waist and knocked him down on his back. I started punching him in the face, but he just laughed as I unleashed a chorus of punches. I grew furious at his mockery. "Why are you laughing?" I asked him, pinning his arms above his head with one hand and pulled out another dagger. I held it at his neck and watched him with annoyance and rage as he kept laughing.

Siddiqis grinned at me, his lip bloody. "I'm laughing at how weak you are. You can't beat me, Rumblen. You can't kill me." He laughed. "Kill me if you're strong enough. I dare you." He stared up at me, cocky and confident. How I hated to be dared.

Rage boiled up inside me and I refused to be mocked. I raised the dagger, its metal shone, and I stared him in the eye. "Good-bye, Siddiqis Starburn." I brought the dagger down.

CHAPTER 36

Weak yet Strong

I SCREAMED IN frustration, when I realized I didn't drive the dagger through Siddiqis; it hovered an inch above his heart. So many thoughts crowded my head. I felt dizzy and my grip loosened on Siddiqis's hands. He grinned up at me. "I told you. You can't kill me because you're too weak."

I jumped off him and threw the dagger back into the belt slot in frustration. I ignored the fact that Siddiqis was on his feet, peering at me curiously. I glared at him with hatred and blinding rage. "I would kill you but it seems too easy. I prefer to hear you scream in pain and die the same way I did." I seethed at him and felt rage boil dangerously in me.

He continued to grin, and I felt stupid for allowing him to breathe. "Give it up, Rumblen. As much as I'd love to hear you continue to rant on about killing me, I have some unfinished business to attend to." He lunged at me, and as I moved out of the way, he slashed a dagger out and cut me across my stomach. He smiled viciously at the slash on my stomach. "Point one for me."

I peered down at the line of fresh blood that appeared on my stomach, feeling rage and a sharp pain, and I looked up just in time to see Siddiqis charge at me again, dagger abandoned. He caught me by the waist, and we went down, him on top of me, and I winced at the impact. But I fought the pain, and soon we were rolling around on the grass, taking turns punching each other and I earned a bloody lip as well, the metallic taste filled my senses.

Siddiqis jumped off the ground and pulled out his crusader sword. It was made like mine except his had no stones on it, only his name craved on the hilt. He held it professionally, in his right hand and grinned at me. "Let's end this with some good old sword fighting, shall we?"

I jumped up and spat out the blood. I pulled out my sword as well, my right hand gripped the hilt and I felt power from the sword surge through me. I lifted up my chin as if to challenge him. "Fine by me."

We took our positions and walked in a circle, eyeing each other. I was good with daggers and sword fighting, but Siddiqis was a swordsman; his skills with the sword were priceless. Fortunately, I spent time practicing sword plays back in my old room at the Mortal Portal and I was as pro as he was. I slowed down my breathing and felt my mother's energy surge through me from the sword, her powers and skills became mine and I was ready to fight. We circled and I took a moment to take in my surroundings. There was a forest across the lake and the battlefield was miles behind me. There were a few tall boulders, but besides that, it was a nice grass area. No one was around to help me and I didn't want help. It was I against Siddiqis, two hybrids, one leaving the field alive and the other soon to be dead forever. Siddiqis looked calm and cocky as always, though he was covered in scratches (I tend to fight dirty by scratching if necessary). I realized we stopped circling. We stared each other down, both of us projecting the hatred we had for each other, and the only sound we heard were the screams of demons and soldiers dying. All of the sudden, Siddiqis lunged at me and I dodged his sword blade as I slashed his forearm. He came at me, ignoring his cut arm, and threw a series of attacks I tried my best to block, though I did get scratched up. He advanced upon me and when I felt he was crossing into my territory, I unleashed attacks of my own and I advanced upon him. We took turns, advancing and retreating, and I got scratched up as well as he did. We were like two salsa dancers, both taking turns advancing and retreating, except we were trying to kill each other. I made an effort to attack for his neck, but he blocked it easily and placed an attack on cheek. I ignored the sharp sting of the cut and I let him advance toward me, so I could lure him toward the boulders.

When I had the right amount of space between us, I jumped backward onto the boulder, and to my dismay, he jumped on the boulder as well and made a swing to behead me, which I dodged by ducking. I scowled at him. "Trying to behead me, are you? Now that's low even for you, is it not?" The clang of the sword's blades making contact rang through my ears. I did a backward flip with a grunt, as I jumped off the boulder and landed on my feet; the impact startled me for a second since I didn't bend my knees before making contact with the ground, and I looked up at a annoyed Siddiqis.

He returned my scowl with one of his own. "I'm not the one running away." He leapt off and landed behind me, a murderous look on his pretty face. "Stop running so I could kill you already." He sounded annoyed as he swung his sword at my stomach and I was quick to spin around and block him as I jumped back.

The swords clanged from the impact and I felt a shuddered creep up my neck. I raised my chin. "I'm not running. I'm just using my resources." I slashed at his chest but he easily deflected it. I blocked his attacks as he advanced and we found ourselves back where we started. He was getting stronger and I struggled to block him. I was growing tired and I felt my defense go down. Before I knew it, Siddiqis hit my sword and the impact caused it to fly out of my grasp. I stared at my empty hand and then at my sword, which was on the grass.

Siddiqis took the opportunity and slashed at my thigh, cutting deep into my flesh, and I cried out in pain. I suddenly felt dizzy and I felt my knees buckle. I fell to the ground, clutching my head in agony. I heard my heart beating faster and faster, and I placed my hands over my heart, trying to slow it down, as I felt a stabbing pain there. I gasped in surprise and pain and placed one hand on the grass, trying to steady myself, while the other hand stayed sprawled over my heart. *What's happening,* I wondered and cried out when the stabbing pain got intense. I grimaced and weakly looked up at Siddiqis, who was grinning down at me in victory.

I narrowed my eyes at him and knew he had done something. "What have you done?" I shouted at him, and my arm that kept my up collapsed and I fell onto my elbow and knees.

Siddiqis laughed. "It worked."

I felt a pang of fear in my and I tried not to panic. "What worked? What did you do?" I looked down, pain displayed on my face but I didn't care how weak I looked. The pain was unbearable.

He gazed upon me in victory and his magenta eyes were dancing with pride. "I poisoned my daggers and sword. I made sure to poison them with poison strong enough to kill anything, including you and I: hybrid poison." He grinned as I looked up shocked. "It seems that you're dying again, Rumblen, but this time, you'll stay dead."

CHAPTER 37

Dying All Over Again

SIDDIQIS TURNED HIS back to me and gazed at the lake, admiring its beauty as I lay behind him in pain. I struggled to stay conscious and I felt the poison slowly mix into my system. Oh God, it pained; the pain was exhilarating. I went cold all over, one of the symptoms of hybrid poison. I withered as the poison continued its work. It was the kind of poison that killed you slowly and I hated that type of poison.

I managed to look up at his back. "You must feel pretty damn good about yourself right now, don't you?" I managed to seethe at him, and I winced as I felt another sharp pain in my heart.

Siddiqis turned around to look at me and smirked as if I had said something funny. "You're actually wrong. I'm feeling pretty damn awesome if I should say so myself." His magenta eyes flashed wickedly and he walked toward me.

I narrowed my eyes at him in disgust. "I can't believe I loved you. You're a monster, a disgrace to our race," I spat out. "I thought you were my lover, but really, you're just a demon hiding behind a cute face." I then cursed myself for admitting he was cute.

He didn't seem to notice. He was too busy peering down at me with an expression I couldn't read. "I'm no monster, my dear Rumblen. I used to be your lover until you broke up with me! I didn't ask for all of this to happen!" His voice rose into a shout and I cringed at the sound. He continued to rant on. "I wanted to have a long life with you and I wanted you to be mine! You ruined our plans, Rumblen. You're the one who started all of this." He gestured toward the battlefield where the battle was slowly dying. "I loved you. I still love you, but if I can't have you, nobody can." He knelt down and tilted my chin up, forcing me to look him in the eyes. His eyes searched mine and I saw my old Siddiqis gazing back at me. He spoke in a softer tone. "Deep down inside of me, I want you to live. I want you to live so you could be mine. And deep down inside of your heart, you love me. You still have feelings for me and I'm going to give you a choice." He cocked his head to the side, inspecting every square inch of my face.

I narrowed my eyes at him, confused. "I don't follow with where you are going with this."

He smiled at me as if I were a clueless child that didn't understand. "My dear Rumblen, I can still save you. You don't have to die. There's still a chance for you to live. Someone has to drain the poison out of your system and give you some blood. If you give me your word that you will love me and be mine, I will save you. It's up to you."

I was silent, having no clue on what to say. I wanted to live. I didn't want to die, but was I really going to bind myself to Siddiqis? I was at crossroads again and the choices were more risky than before. If I said no, then I would die. If I said yes, I would be bounded to a monster that took my old boyfriend's place. Though, I knew it wasn't the monster talking. It was Siddiqis, my Siddiqis. It was the Siddiqis that loved me more than anything, the one I trusted. I realized he was still waiting and I said nothing. How could I? I was on the verge of dying and I knew that if I died, I'd leave my friends in the hands of a psychopath. Then, I saw something scary. I saw my reflection in his eyes and I gasped, stunned. I was going gray. My skin was slowly going colorless, a strand of my hair was turning platinum, and I saw the light fading out of my eyes.

Siddiqis saw as well and his magenta eyes widened. "You're running out of time, Rumblen. Your light is going out and soon it'll be too late to save you."

I was horrified. Nothing had prepared me for that moment. I was never told that when injected with hybrid poison, I would turn gray. I was scared to the bone. I shook my head. "Siddiqis, please. Don't do this." I begged him, desperate. I hated begging but I was dying. I couldn't help but hope he would save me. I hoped my old friend was still there, in that body.

He stared at me, calmly. "Give me your word and I will save you."

I looked him in the eyes, full of fear. "Siddiqis, I'm dying. If you love me, you'd save me even if I didn't give you my word."

He released his hold on my chin, kissed my forehead that sent shivers up my arm, and stood up, his expression grave. "I'm sorry. You lost the chance to save yourself, Rumblen. You have only a few minutes until the poison snuffs out your light." He swiped out a white cloth and wiped his hands, wiping off some blood that may have been his or mine.

I looked down and realized I was crying silent tears. With whatever energy I had, I wiped off the tears that escaped and rolled over on my side and crawled up into a ball, waiting for the end to come. *I failed you, my parents and dear sister,* I apologized silently. *I failed the Mortal Portal and Xercus. I failed my friends. I failed the Deatheye family. I failed to save Siddiqis from himself. I failed myself the most.* I stayed in that ball position and felt the pain intensify. I felt my feet go numb; the poison was numbing my body, starting from the bottom.

I decided to savor my last breath by saying my unspoken words to Siddiqis. "There's something I never told you." My voice was raspy and I had to force the words out.

This caught his attention and he looked down at me. "What didn't you tell me that I didn't already know?"

I looked up at him from my balled up position and smiled weakly. "I never told you when I really fell in love with you."

He narrowed his eyes at me unsure why I was blabbering when I was on the cliff of death. "I never thought of when you started loving me. All I knew was that you did love me."

"Take a guess."

He stood there thinking. "Was it when I threw you into this lake?" He gestured to the great body of water.

I shook my head and instantly regretted it when a headache emerged. "No. I knew I loved you when I broke up our relationship." It was hard admitting it, but I figured I had nothing to lose if I was going to die.

Siddiqis looked confused. "What do you mean? I thought you broke up with me because you didn't love me."

Confusion hit me through the pain and I blinked at him as if I was waking up from a long sleep. "What? I broke up with you because we were going into the final battle of the biggest war we have ever had. I couldn't let emotions distract me so I called our relationship off," I explained. "I always loved you, Siddiqis. I knew right when you left my room, heartbroken, that I was in love with you. I turned off my feelings to focus on the battle, and when it ended, I turned them back on. Of course, I told myself not to think about you, but do you know how hard it was when I saw you at your welcoming party? I tried not to love you and you're right. I still love you. But I also love Gustav. I was destined for him to keep balance between the countries. But now that doesn't matter. I'm dying. I guess we're even." I looked up at him and saw he was shocked at my words.

Siddiqis cocked his head at me, eyes wide. "What do you mean we're even?"

I smiled, suddenly feeling tired. "You killed me and I came back to life. I broke your heart and now, you're stopping mine." I dropped my head back onto the dry grass and tried to sleep before I died. I sighed. "I guess this is a better way. At least I'll be sleeping when I die." I closed my eyes, shielding everything out.

He was quiet and then, he knelt down beside my curled up body. He took my hands in his and I let him. His warm touch sent delightful shivers up my arm and I sighed at the feeling. Even with my eyes closed, I could feel Siddiqis's gaze on me. My legs were starting to get numb when he spoke. "Tell me. If I wasn't like this, if I wasn't so bad, would you have loved me?"

I didn't even hesitate to say the answer. "Yes. I would. And I still do. You're right. We are destined to be together forever." I opened my eyes, peering at him. Our faces were inches apart and I could smell his minty breath mixed with his sweat and blood. "Kiss me good night," I whispered, tilting my head up to kiss him.

He slowly broke the gap between us and kissed me long and pleasurably. It was an enticing kiss, a kiss full of love and sorrow at the same time. He closed his eyes, moaning, and deepened the kiss while I drew my hands away from him. He caressed my cheeks with one hand and the other hand kept me off the ground. It was a beautiful good-bye kiss, and I felt my old friend kissing me again the way he used to. He was a great kisser; his kisses are long, dirty, and pleasurable. It was too bad that it was the last kiss we'd have. With him distracted in the kiss, my plan was in place.

I smiled while we were kissing, moving his lips with mine as I spoke, and I held one of my daggers in my hand firmly. "I'm sorry, my dear." Before he could react, I pushed him away with all of the energy I had left, making him fall on his butt, and I drove the dagger through him, right in the middle of his heart. Now, we were even.

CHAPTER 38

Never Going Down Alone

HE GASPED FROM pain and shock, looking down at the dagger's hilt that stuck out of his chest. He knew it wasn't an ordinary dagger. It was an enchanted dagger, which meant it could kill him. He stared at me, stunned. "What have you done?" he whispered, his magenta eyes wide with shock and blind rage. He would have attacked me if I hadn't stabbed him through his heart.

I looked at him and smiled sweetly. "Don't take it personally. I meant every word I said. Including when I said we are destined to be together forever. If I go down, you go down with me." I fell to my side again and stared at him, smiling dazzled.

Siddiqis clawed at the dagger's hilt, desperate to free it out of his body. Giving up after realizing it was too deep, he stared at me with raging magenta eyes. "You tricked me. I can't believe it. I can't die! There's no way!" He looked around, frantically for help, but we were all alone.

I chuckled darkly, and there was no humor behind it. "I thought the same thing when you killed me."

He fell to his side as well, his head near my feet and my head near his feet. We were like the ying and yang symbol; the two of us kept each other in place, one bad side and a good side. He looked at me, his head rested on the grass, and he was breathing hard. "This can't be. No, no, no, no, no, no, no," he moaned. He truly was crushed and I couldn't help but smile at his misery.

I stared at him, a smirk on my face. "I guess it's the end for both of us now, Siddiqis." My voice was raspy and my throat felt like sandpaper; each time I talked, it felt like sandpaper rubbing together.

His breathing started to slow and I knew that in a blink of the eye, he would be a dead man. But on his last breath, he whispered something that chilled my blood. "I will be back for you and I will have my revenge," he swore. And like that, he was gone. Dead. His eyes were still open, their magenta color faded, and he lay there on his side, looking at me with dead cold eyes. I saw a promise for vengeance in them.

I didn't realize I was crying until I felt hot tears stream down my cheeks. "Good-bye, Siddiqis Starburn," I whispered. I then decided to send him off with the same prayer he sang for me. "*My brother, my blood. May he lay his head. May the dirt of the past become his bed. May he rest in peace; his soul will be free. And May the Angel and Satan let him be.*" After, I closed my own eyes and waited. My hands were tingling; they were the next to go numb. I listened to the sounds of the battle and I knew that we were victorious even though I was dying. I was wrong. I didn't fail. I killed the threat and that's what mattered. I was calm and I stayed there for twenty minutes.

* * *

Finally, I heard footsteps running toward me. By now, my arms were numb and the numbness was spreading to my stomach, close to my heart. I kept my eyes closed as the footsteps neared and then knew the figure saw me. "Rumblen!" the figure shouted.

I opened my eyes, weakly, when I recognized that voice. It was Gustav. "Over here," I croaked, my voice raspy because my throat was awfully dry.

He ran to me and he fell to his knees in front of me. "Oh, Rumblen," he moaned. "What happened?" He had blood on his hands and on his face that made him look tougher than he was. His piercing blue eyes were clouded with concern. "Oh god." His eyes widened at the sight of me turning gray. He cupped my face in his hands and peered at me with desperation.

I smiled weakly. "Hey." It was a weak thing to say, but I knew I was going to die. I wanted so badly to close my eyes again.

Gustav shook his head. "Don't die on me. Stay awake. What do I have to do? Tell me!" He shook me by the shoulders to keep me awake.

I shook my head, still smiling. "It's useless. My light's going out. I'm beyond help."

"Don't tell him that, Kyra," a familiar voice said.

I looked toward the sound to see a woman hovering beside him. She was shimmering, which gave away the fact that she was an angel. She had dark curly waves streaming past her shoulders and she was slightly skinny. Her skin was fair and her eyes were an enticing dark gray. She looked exactly like me, but older and she had a softer look while I looked tough. She was beautiful, a true angel like the one that restored Gustav's heart beat. It then struck me that I knew her. My eyes widened in disbelief. "Luna," I whispered.

Gustav shook his head. "No, Rumblen. It's me." He couldn't see her.

Luna smiled down at me and then looked at his son. "Don't tell him I'm here. I wanted to talk to you, Kyra." Her smile filled me with love.

I started to cry, hot tears streamed down my graying face. "I missed you so much, Luna. Why didn't you ever visit me?" I was so happy to see her, but I was confused on why she decided to visit me when I was dying.

She smiled sadly. "Oh, Kyra, I wanted to visit you. But I had to take care of something. Now I need you to listen to me, all right?" She sounded like herself when she was alive.

I nodded, happy to hear her soft voice again. "Okay."

"Rumblen, what's happening?" Gustav asked, confused about whom I was talking to. I ignored him.

"Kyra, you have to tell Gustav how to save you," Luna said.

I scrunched my eyebrows in confusion. "But I'm dying."

"I know, but he could save you before it's too late," she argued, her deep gray eyes filled with concern.

I stared at her, unsure. "Are you sure? What if it doesn't work?"

"It will work. Trust me, Kyra. When have I ever let you down?" She smiled at me, her pearl white teeth shone like the star she gave me.

I nodded, trusting her words, and turned my gaze back to Gustav. "Gustav, in order to save me, you have to get the poison out of me and then you have to give me some of your blood." My voice came out uneven.

Gustav nodded. "All right." He located a vein on my wrist, cutting it open, and pressed his lips on my skin. He started to suck the poison out and after five minutes, he spitted out a mouthful of black blood. The cut on my wrist was closed up. Then, he held his own wrist up to my mouth. "Drink," he urged and I did. I was hungry and weak.

My fangs shot out and I sank them into his vein, causing him to wince slightly but he didn't pull away. Blood tastes and smells like old pennies in reality, but to a vamp, it smells and tastes like fresh cherries. Gustav's blood tasted so sweet I closed my eyes, savoring the taste. Its rich taste was enticing and the flow was heavenly. It had been so long since I had fed on anybody or even had blood. Gustav moaned in pleasure and I knew that it was because when I fed, I made the person I fed on feel soothed, as if they weren't being bitten. I drank and drank until I felt myself heal.

Then, I let go and sank back against the grass, and I felt my breathing slow down. Slowly, I raised my arm and peered at it. I smiled when I saw my color returning and the numbness was gone. I felt energy surge through me, and I looked up at Gustav, who was beaming.

He pulled me into a long hug and I sighed happily against his body. It wasn't until we pulled away I saw that he was crying. "Never leave me again. Swear you won't." God, he looked so damn serious but sounded so close to breaking. The fact that he loved me so much just made me swell up with tears.

I laughed, tears of joy filled my eyes, and nodded. Then, I was kissing him, expressing my love through the kiss. I didn't die. I was alive. Thanks to him. I broke our embrace and smiled at him radiantly. "We won."

He nodded, smiling as well. "We won," he repeated. Then, he looked taken back. "What's this?" He reached toward my hair and pulled a small amount, so I could see it.

I gasped. It was platinum, standing out through my dark waves. I reached up and brought the hair closer to my eyes. It was bold and I knew hair dye wouldn't solve the problem. I looked at Gustav and back to my now platinum streak. "Jesus, I'm not that old."

Gustav laughed. "I know. I guess you're stuck with that," he added. "But don't worry. I still love you even if you have a silver streak."

I scowled at him, but failed because I laughed as well. "It's not silver. It's platinum!" I decided to make it a fashion statement, though I was sure no one would follow it. I turned my gaze to my old friend.

Luna smiled and the sun seemed to beam brighter, as a halo shone above her head. I then stared in awe at her. I must have been her assignment because now that I won the battle, she was a guardian angel. She noticed the halo as well and beamed down at me. "What's done is done. You have my blessings, Kyra. I must go now but I promise I'll visit again, Kyra. I give you my word." Then she disappeared and I couldn't help but feel sadden. Though she would keep her word. I knew she would.

I looked at Siddiqis's limp body and my smile got smaller. "I killed him." It came out as a whisper, barely came out actually.

Gustav looked at his body and was expressionless. "It's all right. You had to."

I started shaking when I remembered Siddiqis's last words. "Gustav, he swore he would have revenge. Does that mean – " I couldn't finish the sentence, afraid that even finishing would bring him back from the dead.

He shook his head, his expression serious and his tone promising. "He's dead, Rumblen. You're free."

I nodded, believing him, and leaned toward Siddiqis's body. I closed his dead eyes. *Good-bye, Siddiqis Starburn,* I thought, hoping he had heard. I felt pride well up inside of my heart and I knew why. I won. I fulfilled my destiny and made my parents, Luna, and my sister proud. I was right all along. I left the field alive while Siddiqis stayed there dead and to rot.

CHAPTER 39

Still Alive

AFTER A FEW minutes, Gustav and I both trotted into the battlefield. The stench of demon flesh filled my nostrils and the sight was as horrible as the smell. Decays of demons laid, ashes were on the ground, and the worst part was that the ground was littered with some bodies of soldiers. I flinched at the sight of one Xercus soldier that was covered in blood, dead, and I knew that one of the demons must have been craving flesh. With Gustav supporting me, we walked through and stopped. Aries, Darq, Bonzai, Angela, and Boota stood together, talking. They were all scratched up and they hadn't noticed us from where we stood. The sight of my friends alive made me cry silently, tears of relief streamed down my face.

Finally, Angela saw me and squealed with delight. She ran toward me and knocked all of the air out of my lungs in a big hug. I hugged her back tightly, both of us crying happily. When we pulled away, she smiled. "We won! We kicked those demons to the curb!" She had a deep slash on her forehead that promised a scar and she was covered in burns, showing me that she was messing with some fire-breathing demons. But she couldn't care less about her injuries. She started doing a victory dance, hopping from one foot to another. I couldn't help but smile. Angela took the death of demons a little too joyous.

Darq and Boota stood together, smiling at me. Darq had a slash across his cheek and he had a makeshift bandage around his left arm. But it was Boota that I was worried about. She was covered in scratches and she had a white cloth around her leg that was soaked in blood. Even though she was in a critical condition, she beamed at me with pride and leaned her head into the groove of Darq's neck, his arm around her waist. I knew that I shouldn't have worried about Boota; Darq would never let anything horrible happen to her. Darq flashed me a thumbs-up and smiled down at Boota who was peering at me as if I were an angel.

I switched my gaze to Aries, who was grinning at me with pride and relief. He glanced over at Darq and Boota and then did a double take at them, eye wide with blind shock. *Oh lord, this won't go well,* I thought, chuckling quietly and so did Gustav and Angela. I had no idea how the two would explain themselves but I knew they'd find a way. Finally, it took all of my guts to peer at Bonzai.

He stared at me, shocked. Then he took longs steps toward me and engulfed me into an embrace. I took in his body heat and started to cry, realizing how happy I was to see him. We pulled away and tears were fresh in his beautiful green eyes. "You're alive," he said, relief in his voice. "I was so scared we lost you, but then Darq told me that you were alive and we were going to battle. Are you all right?"

I nodded, taking him in and the sight of him made happiness bloom through my heart.

Concern clouded his green eyes and he searched my face. It took him a while to see that my eyes were both a different color than the other, as well as the platinum streak in my dark hair. When he finally saw both changes, he started sputtering out questions, which I was quick to wave off, promising to answer them later and I did.

I looked around at all of my friends. *Not friends, family,* I corrected myself. I turned my full gaze to Aries. "I did it. I killed Siddiqis." I tried to say it in a strong voice but it barely came out as a whisper. "No more problems."

Aries nodded, as if he had known. He stopped trying to wipe off the blood on his hands and gazed at me. The look that he gave me told me that I was wrong. "Kyra, we have one more issue."

Angela groaned. "Are you kidding me? And I really thought that we all were having a perfect normal moment!" She threw her hands in the air as if to say, *Seriously?*

Aries shook his head and seemed a little disturbed. "It's not that big of an issue. Fine, maybe it is. But I don't know if I should bring it up."

Darq, Gustav, Angela, Boota, Gustav, and I gawked at him. I had never heard the powerful Aries so unsure before. Gustav scrunched his eyebrows at his father with confusion and impatience. "Father, please tell us."

I nodded at Aries. "It's all right. Please tell us." The suspense was just killing me.

Aries sighed. "It's noth – "

"Oh, just tell us!" Angela interrupted, frustrated and I knew she hated waiting.

Aries stared me dead in the eye as he spoke. "There's still the matter that made us end up here." Seeing my confused expression, he grew more serious and finally blurted it out. "Kyra, you still have to choose who will you marry."

Boota inhaled, sharply.

Angela gasped.

The three Deatheye boys went still as statues while I registered what Aries had said. And when I finally did, I thought, *Shoot.*

I felt my heart stop for a full three seconds and then it started back again beating faster and faster, as if I had just ran in a marathon. I could barely talk and I managed to say, "Oh, that's right." I looked from Darq, who was looking very uncomfortable, to Bonzai, who seemed taken back, to Gustav, who was staring at me with longing that took my heart away. *Oh lord, I totally forgot about that,* I wondered. I cleared my throat. "Well, I guess this is pretty awkward." *Gustav, Gustav, Gustav,* a voice in my head whispered. I shushed that voice and realized I knew all along whom I wanted to marry from the moment we kissed, that spark we felt the first time. "Getting married means commitment. And I know there's one person that I'd want to live with for my entire life." I closed my eyes, hoping my heart wasn't going to fail me. I took in a big breath and gathered all of my courage as I turned to face Gustav, who was staring at me with a wanting gaze. Love literally floated off him and I knew that my heart was right.

I smiled at him. "I choose Gustav Deatheye. I want to spend my every waking moment with him until I die. Of course, if he wants the same." I peered at him, praying he'll say yes.

Gustav appeared astonished, blue eyes wide, and then he turned to Aries whom was gazing at his son with fatherly pride. "Father?"

Aries smiled and nodded. "It's up to you, son." He really was a softy after all because he was tearing up.

Gustav nodded and turned back at me, his icy blue eyes pierced my soul with love. He smiled and took my hands in his, gazing into my eyes with admiration. He didn't even hesitate. "Yes, I will marry you Kyra Rumblen Count." Then, he started tearing up and his voice gave away how overjoyed he was when he said, "I love you." He pulled me into a hug, our bodies pressed together securely.

I felt everything inside of me burst into a river of love and I hugged my fiancé tightly with a ridiculous smile on my face.

We both started laughing, and finally, Gustav pulled away to kiss me full on the lips, knowing that everyone was watching though he didn't care. I'm pretty sure I was blushing, but I was also wooed by the love impacted behind the kiss.

When we pulled away, we stared each other dead in the eye, not saying a word because our love was too radiant to express through words. I looked around at everyone's expressions. Angela was teary-eyed, Boota and Darq were beaming and crying silently with joy as they clutched each other, Aries stared at us with pride, and Bonzai was smiling, as though he had understood that Gustav was the right choice over him. I smiled at that moment. *Finally, I can live in peace*, I thought with a happy sigh. From that day on, I was Kyra Rumblen Deatheye, daughter of Lilith Demonheart and Curtis Count, daughter-in-law of Aries Deatheye and Luna Deatheye, and Gustav Deatheye's wife. That was the day I fulfilled my destiny and I couldn't have been happier. Like every fairytale, we lived happily ever after. The end. Or is it?

EPILOGUE

One Year Later

MY HANDS HOVERED over the laptop keyboard as I thought of what to write next. The story was done; there was nothing left but the future, which I couldn't see. Behind me, the bedroom door opened and closed with a slam and a sigh followed afterward. I smiled, knowing whom it was even before I turned around in my chair. My husband smiled at me and I knew by the dark circles under his eyes that he's tired. "Hey," I greeted softly and then turned my full attention back to the screen.

Gustav groaned and walked to me. "Can you please stop staring at that damn screen? You've been typing for days now! And why aren't you ready?" He rubbed his jaw, his blue eyes flashed with impatience.

It was true. I had been so caught up with writing that I had forgotten all about Althaea's, Angela's sister's, birthday that started at 3:00 p.m. I smacked my forehead. "Shoot! I totally forgot! What time is it?"

"Two p.m."

I said a very inappropriate word that Gustav laughed at and jumped out of the chair. I gave him a quick kiss and headed for the shower.

After taking a quick hot shower, I emerged out of the bathroom in a midnight blue strapless short party dress with a single blue rose tied along the waist, my hair down and dark as the night except for the platinum strand I had, a reminder of the battle I had won. I pulled on a pair of stilettos that matched my dress color and looked up just in time to see Gustav in front of the mirror, trying to put on his tie.

I smiled at his frustration and went to help him. I smiled up at him. "How was the meeting?"

Gustav sighed dramatically. "I never knew how rude hobgoblins were. I almost threw a stapler at the leader of the Servic Clan!" He scowled as if bringing up the memory disgusted him.

I laughed at him and I knew why he's so stressed out. He had to attend all of the meetings with the Clans and he hated it when some of the Clans were rude. I finished his tie and gave him a kiss on the cheek. "Suck it up, buttercup." I walked to the door, opened it, and closed it behind me as I entered the hallway.

It was a year since the last battle, and ever since then, I had been living in the Xercus castle and sleeping in the second master's bedroom that looks like the one where my father-in-law sleeps in. At that time, Aries was out of the country to hold a meeting with the Servic Royal Family and wasn't coming back until a week, and Bonzai was off with his gorgeous wife on their honeymoon, so Gustav and I had the castle all to us. Darq and Boota moved out the year before, after the war, so the two could enjoy a normal life together and the two were so happy. They were even happier when they learned they're going to be parents of a beautiful boy. I still had no idea what they told Aries, but apparently they got his blessings and Boota's parents' blessings as well. Everything was fine and everyone was happy, including me.

I walked down the hall and I reached the top of the stairs, when a knock came from the front door. I narrowed my eyes at the door. "Who is it?" I called.

The silence was piercing. No answer.

I sauntered down the stairs and stopped at the bottom. I looked around cautiously. *Who could that be?* I wondered. I knew that it was a male, from how hard he knocked and I decided that I shouldn't go close to the door, in case the person knocking was a threat. I raised my right hand, and using telekinesis, I unlocked the door. I took in a deep breath. "It's open." I called, waiting for the visitor to enter.

The door swung open and closed behind the figure and it took me a while to see the figure was wearing a very antique cloak with the hood up, masking his face. The cloak was long and a dusty brown, but it didn't cover what he wore underneath: black war gear with bloodstains. I flinched at the sight of the deep wound over his heart and then it hit me. *A wound over his heart? Doesn't that mean this man is dead?* I wondered as I stared at this stranger. "Who are you?" I asked, holding my posture straight.

The figure took off his hood and his face hit the light. My heart dropped. *No,* I thought, *No, no, no, no, no, this isn't possible.* "Y-You?" I stuttered, fear and panic rose up inside of me. I took in his scratched face and the dried blood on his face. He had dried blood in his hair and he smelled decayed. Even though he looked gruesome, his charm stood out more than ever. His piercing magenta eyes struck me like lightning.

Siddiqis grinned like the devil he was. "Hello, Rumblen. Did you miss me?" He grinned, his teeth showing, and I saw that they were razor sharp like a piranha's and pieces of flesh were noticeable. He was alive, right there in the castle. A memory flashed before my eyes: myself plunging an enchanted dagger through Siddiqis's heart.

He eyed me. "Don't you remember what I said right before I died? C'mon, think really hard." His eyes gleamed wickedly and I fought the urge to run to Gustav.

I didn't have to think because I already knew. His words had haunted me since then. I spoke with a strong voice even though I was on the verge of fainting. "'I will be back for you and I will have my revenge.'" I shook my head. "I don't get it. You can't be alive. I killed you myself!"

Siddiqis smirked. "I died, yes. But I came back to life the same way you did." He stepped toward me and reflexively, I stepped back only to be stopped by the stairs. Then he gave it a thought. "Well, sort of like that."

I narrowed my eyes at him, confused. "I broke a curse."

He smiled. "Yes, you did."

"Then, how are you still alive?"

"You broke my curse and there is the matter of the new Prophecy."

I gawked at him, shocked. There was no way I broke his curse. "What curse? And what's the Prophecy this time?" I dared to ask, wanting to know so bad the suspense was just killing me. The last Prophecy meant I had to kill Siddiqis, so what was this one?

Siddiqis grinned. "My curse was: *The day the hybrid loses a loved one is the day that the hybrid becomes the sinner and only death will bring humanity back to that hybrid.*"

I gasped when I realized what curse that was. "The hybrid love curse."

He stared at me with intensity. "The day you killed me, my curse was broken and I have you to thank."

I got that through my head and felt dizzy. "And the new Prophecy?"

His grin faltered. "*The sinner must take his place beside The Chosen Hybrid, for both are a whole.*" When he saw my confused expression, he sighed. "It means that you and I are one."

I shook my head. "What do you mean, we are one? You think we are a whole?"

He quickly closed the gap between us and I didn't dare step back. He stared down at me. "I don't think. I *know.*"

I stared up at him and felt something bubble up inside of me. I realized it wasn't fear. It was anger. Before my brain could react, I shoved him with both hands square in the chest, sending him flying into a wall. He hit it hard and fell to his side, sputtering out blood. I felt a sharp pain in my side as he hit the floor. It was so painful I fell down to the floor on my side, and I couldn't breathe from some kind of impact. It felt like *I* was the one who was hurled into a wall. I shouted in pain. I realized with a gasp he was right. I felt his pain. Him and I were a whole. We were bounded.

"Rumblen!" someone shouted.

I heard someone running down the stairs to me and I looked up to see Gustav kneeling beside me, his icy blue eyes full of worry.

He checked my pulse and sighed of relief when he got a steady pulse. He helped me up to my feet and squinted at me. "What happened?"

I pointed to where Siddiqis was, who was recovered and on his feet as well, staring at both of us.

Gustav turned to look at him and his face with pale. Then, he went red with rage. He started to walk toward him, but I grabbed his arm.

I gazed at his confused expression. "Gustav, we've got a problem." I looked at Siddiqis who nodded at me with a solemn look. "A big problem."

To be continued.

Next Book:

A Prophecy